For Alice

1

The 'Velvet Revolution' lingers downtown in the cobbled pastel streets. In the suburbs, it's as if these things have been ignored, as suburbs generally are. Except there's the above ground commuter train—clean, efficient signature of Soviet Communism's best accomplishments. It must have carried the citizens, hearts beating, into the old city for what might be the most gentle taking down of an empire in recorded history. Pride and optimism permeate the air along with a certain naivety in the memorial bed of bouquets, candles and an odd trodden shoe by Wenceslas Square.

And so Maebh Murray feels for once in her life - a foreigner working in a foreign land - that she is where she should be. On the fringe but just touching—hoping only to be caught up in whatever, wherever it might take her. The job gives feigned purpose and she is as set as this newly defined nation on ideals and a future that comes without a compass. It's spring 1990. She's twenty-three and just out of university. Czechoslovakia needs English teachers. Sure, she'll do that; and here she is. Their Cold War is over and hers is at hand.

She walks home from the train in the evening. The butterflies graze the weedy grasses. A man is flirting with a bevy of girls. He wears an odd suit and a goatee as might an intellectual or a waiter. She seems not to look like a tourist and he seems to call her over in Czech but is not impressed she can't speak his language.

"Are you an idiot?" Some expressions defy translation and the girls laugh.

She passes them by—a shadow on the pavement, almost tall, fragile but resilient. She must take herself down, the walls let in to pluck and frame. Beautiful inside and out, they say, but that doesn't protect her much, not even from herself. Amidst the park of buildings, the earth is already dry and she holds spring's imminent flowers in daisy chains round her person. She writes poems: she is a poem—walking on miracles, beckoning tragedies her way. She has been let loose on the world and though it doesn't seem likely, she feels her collapse already.

She will meet a man and marry him knowing he will hurt her. She will have a child too, still one herself.

The scars on her person she never knew existed, will be etched out. She will watch their magnificence stretch over the wrinkled bed sheets and, thus haloed, make of herself a subject in her own destiny. A carelessly crafted, wrecked life is careful in its way and something, at least, to hold with curiosity and defiance, in one's hands. She hasn't much idea what else to do with life but experience the almost absence of it. The spot where one clings to a crevice wanting both to hang on and just let go.

The building where she's staying holds itself empty. It is a building among buildings, box housing for all—faceless concrete warriors holding down the threat of elitism in its cemetery. In the building, she takes the stairs up. An evening rose wades the foyer and bare walls till the front door closes behind her. There is an elevator, but then she couldn't get away if necessary, or out if it jammed. A few scab scuffs mark up the walls but otherwise it's sterile. One at a time quick, two at a time slow—five or six flights depending on whether first floor means ground or one above ground. It's not that anyone is there—suburban Prague is staid for a stabbing but you feel eyes on you more in strange places.

She watches her own irresolution.

The people in this building, whatever kind live here, must have gone off to old-age summer camp like Frantisek's grandmother. The woman whose apartment they have given her to stay in. She puts all the plastic nick-nacks in the closet till it's barren and not pretending to be otherwise. Fake flowers, especially those most cherished, are sadder where they won't grow. The empty beds running between the chipped paths below and the veiled curtains indifferent above. All coated with a dimness that sniffles out history, violence, breath. Balconies open from every second window and that kind of regu-

larity is not what she fancies peering in, although it is no more orderly than the books she has in one pile to read.

She heads straight to the kitchen except first she stands backed up against the front door watching the bread knife on the kitchen table. No creature comes in to grab it in all the minutes she holds this position. As if her life, or any other, is important. And then a creature would be company to get her through the evening but there's no handsome stranger there. She remembers cutting up bread to eat with butter and jam before setting out that morning which she enjoyed so she's not depressed. On the surface, she's in bloom and although there is too much of a something flitting about her eyes, when not drawn in, she shines.

She takes three steps to the fridge and opens it angled in such a way she might see anyone watching behind her. Too aware of each step she takes, she can't seem to come out of the cut-out doll she's pasted on or erase herself from a landscape that ignores her. Anonymity remains illusive, even in this emptiness.

She pours some red juice into a glass and tops it with water. Then she rips off some bread to eat with the ham and mayonnaise salad filled with peas and things. She's used to better fare but is not missing it as much as she might. The salad is one of the few dishes she has found to eat here along with the roast chicken downtown, which keeps going up in price. She buys the salad at the company lunch shop. The girls in the shop seem unhappy with her. Her salary is unreasonably high and she was supposed to eat with the executives, but one day, after the stewed fatty meat and dumplings, she fainted in front of everyone. The picked-over food tray splayed about disdaining the hierarchy of things.

She curls up on the sofa-bed in the main room for the evening with her salad. The books, notepads and pens are on the coffee table with the writers' names scrawled out in various fonts—Kafka, Joyce, a bilingual edition of Dante's *Purgatorio.* She's determined to cover the whole canon but she should be reading Virginia, both Emilys, and Simone, too. Except, she doesn't know that yet and is afraid to find women writers wanting of something other than the patriarchy that held them back. However, she calls them by their first names as though familiar with them already.

Can women even go there—make a shape of existence, adhered with beauty and cruelty resonating through?

—

When Maebh first arrived, she stayed at a student residence. Her roommate had a wigged kerchief over her head and was recovering from an illness but there were cornflowers in her face. She sang "My Bonnie Lies Over the Ocean" as if that were the only English she knew and all she loved overseas. She had tears in her eyes, so relieved she seemed of company, but the next morning she was gone and Maebh had the rooms to herself to count the hours she had never had to before. Loneliness in a crowded house had been no stranger but it was the silence. She had lived —the furniture sometimes sticky with gooseberry jam and wine spills—hiding in corners by the goings back and forth of roommates, a boy-friend, parents and three siblings and she must have enjoyed this more than she realized. She had never lived alone with white walls and sunny pine furniture so she snuck Dubi in after hours that night he was in town.

Dubi was teaching at an ammunition factory in Zlín. Of the whole planeload who came over from The University of Toronto, Maebh was the one to get the post in Prague and that bit of luck made her hopeful luck might hold.

"I can't take another weekend there," Dubi said, "and they'll never know." But then Dubi is here recovering from a heroin addiction. He twisted up the spare bed irreparably and the residence maid was a spy. Maebh came home to find her key opened only the one room in the suite. It was a no male visitors place, but that Dubi was not up for tussling with girls, meant nothing to them.

Frantisek and the director of the residence called her into the office. Maebh thought she would get a scolding but:

"We hope you will feel at home in Prague," the director said smiling.

He was not bearded like Frantisek but seemed as romantic and to believe, as her employers, that she'd come not on a whim but to help them.

"Would you like to stay at my grandmother's apartment?" Frantisek asked. "I think you'll feel more free there."

Freedom was his favourite word and he was avid about the lack of it during the Soviet occupation.

"I wanted to be a Reverend but the government said I had to study Computer Programming," he explained on the subway over.

"I wanted to do graduate school," Maebh replied, "but worked so many hours waitressing to pay tuition and rent I never got the grades." But that doesn't cover it. She had been raised in scorn of academic effort.

"You either have it or you don't," dad had said that time he mocked her high average and all the time she spent in her room when she should have been kicking the establishment. "And women generally don't. They can do business and stuff but are just not cut out for genius."

Her father, of course, knew the canon—dates, writers and texts by heart—and had at some point put in the hours. "They don't become serial killers either," he had added as if to make it more palatable but it didn't. A licence to be bad is as liberating as a licence to be great and the chance to choose between the two even more so.

Maebh liked staying up late with him and his wine glass, though, till he fell asleep, head lolling at an impossible angle. He could talk about *Othello*, the Moors, injustice and roll it all up with string theory as dense as a black hole. But she only ever got those marks once—the kind that get you scholarships. Maybe he just didn't want her to know as much as he did and she doesn't, not by a long shot, if knowing is a countable noun. It was poor form, seemingly, in Ireland to follow too closely in the footsteps of your forefathers. Having benefitted from their experience, you ran the risk of showing them up.

"But your parents had two cars and a big house?" Frantisek asked.

"They did but sometimes we slept in the basement and had to rent out the rooms upstairs," she told him, and of how her father had driven his Porsche for one year before it was left in the backyard with the weeds.

"He racked up too many parking tickets and then after the late-'80's market crash they only had the light green Renault 5."

But Frantisek brushed this off in a confusion Maebh felt certain indicated that the recently liberated Eastern bloc had no idea of the rougher conditions many lived by under the "freedom" of democracy they glorified. Not of course that she really got it either, growing up chi-chi bohemian in a few different sandblasted Victorians in Cabbagetown, a gentrifying neighbourhood in Toronto squished between two housing estates. The long time depraved walked up Parliament Street, past health food shops they never frequented. The last house had a burgundy Ikea kitchen her father had picked up from the "as is" section and her mother, all Lancôme eye pencils and mauve silk shirts, had put up the *For Sale* sign with her name on it before they moved back to Ireland again. The house stood stately on the corner with one of those charming turret balconies. No one had ever sat there but the idea was enough. That's what charm is.

—

Priya, Frantisek's wife, was waiting for them at his grandmother's apartment when Frantisek brought her here. She wore a red mini skirt, yellow camisole with no bra, and nylons over legs with dark matted hairs. Her complexion glowed and Frantisek looked so proud of her.

"Only prostitutes shave their legs here," she said as Maebh wondered what to do with the stubble on hers. She hadn't been able to find a waxing salon but perhaps a desire for smooth legs had set her up for a looser life than she'd expected having become sexually active a bit late in life. She had had a hard time connecting with anyone and could have held off longer but had decided to bear through it with someone she pretended to love. For years she had feared opening up to experiences she knew would disappoint even if she had known how to set them in motion and how to even define exactly what she liked.

Priya smoothed the sheets down on the bed and Frantisek struggled to put the duvet into its cover so she helped him.

"That's why I have a wife," he said looking at his hands with the same helplessness as Maebh's father so she whipped the duvet through the air a little harder than necessary.

Priya had come to Prague from Kerala for university and she and Frantisek spoke the best English in the company where she taught. Unlike her husband, however, she was happy to be working in computer science. Communism hadn't unburdened women of domestic labour but at least it had given them jobs.

"It's okay," she said looking up adoringly at her husband. "Men will be men."

Maebh buttoned up the duvet cover as calmly as she could. She envied Priya as she had envied her mother. They were able to contend with a loving *he makes the big bucks husband* and their own *li'l job* money.

"When is Quebec going to get its freedom," asked Priya to turn the mood around.

"It's not that easy to cut places up. There are the aboriginal communities and various cultural and religious groups all over Canada just as there are Gypsies and you here," Maebh said trying to point out that, like Quebec, Prague was more multicultural than the Czechs realized.

"You Canadians cannot possibly understand," she said.

"Well, I'm Irish too," she said. "And I think we both know what cut up looks like."

"Maybe but you could be gentler," she said. "Change takes time! And you are so harsh on our boss. He pays you well and is only doing his job."

Maebh blushed. The president of the company had hoped she'd give him private lessons but withdrew when he saw her distaste for his slicked back hair and business speak. She had tried to hide it but he fawned so over Western Culture which only increased her scorn.

"You have such an old rich culture here," Maebh said, "English and democracy are no panacea."

"We can try," Priya said. "Or never break the chain."

"Fleetwood Mac," Maebh said laughing. Many of her students spoke like this having learnt English from listening to music.

"Yes," said Priya. "I played it everyday for a while."

"Me too," said Maebh.

They moved into the kitchen and Priya showed her all the cherry jam in the pantry.

"Are there any foods I shouldn't eat because of the radiation from Chernobyl?" she asked.

"We eat everything," Priya shrugged, "and lose a few years off our lives."

Again, Maebh felt checked by her wisdom and when she had the keys to the apartment in hand and turned the bolt on the door after Priya and Frantisek left, she felt lost.

—

Maebh teaches everyone in the company from the cleaners and cooking staff to the lab-coat computer scientists and socializes with them more than she expects to. It is like being part of a community and this was another thing she had never experienced. Still, she spent many evenings alone wishing someone was there. Community was nice but she was more of a one-at-a -time person and finding that one person she could talk to forever had never been easy. She usually found she had little to say after a while to the people she thought she knew, but there must be someone she could speak to longer.

She meets other tourists in town and brings a few back—she's more afraid of being alone with herself than with men she'd never met. One guy smelled too heavily of cigarettes and his droopy bum felt disconnected from the rest of him. Another was sculpted like a stunted David statue but when they got to underwear and the Pilsner buzz wore off, the banal in his gym-powered chest brought out the same in his face. She pushed him out the door before he could take more off. The doctor at the hospital where they took her when she fainted had glossy hair swept back over his crown. He had said he wanted lessons but she had just removed a pair of white rubber boots and a bunch of suction sensors from her mostly naked self. It's not that she always says no. At a Friday night sleepover party with her students, the Slavic looking fellow she had been flirting with slipped past the other sleeping bodies onto her and then inside her and she lay as cold as she had with the knife on the table. And this only made it last longer.

"It's okay, you can have your princess from faraway lands," his wife might have said, "but just once." The Czechs are liberal that way.

This ruined things with the man who took her to pretty parks out of town. He held her breast when she cried but she didn't understand sweet.

—

Maebh still hasn't the courage to get undressed. Not that it is fear but something duller. She creeps to the bathroom to spread the wild rose cleanser over her face. She's like mum but blue eyed, thinner and shorter by almost an inch as she is constantly told. She takes care of herself too—the part that could age anyway. Her sometime beauty in the mirror surprises her but then she is more suspicious of it than her mum especially as it wipes off with a cotton swab and warm water. Her complexion along the T-zone turns ruddy and her presence mousy. Beauty flicks on like a light bulb but then it is nice to have the option of downplaying it in defence. She might even destroy it as an experiment, not wanting it to be most of all what she is about.

She heads back to the couch bed and pulls up the sheets over her, dress and all.

The couch at home was Art Shoppe grey velvet and rust velvet curtains hung round the bay window. The Persian rugs were worn and everyone put their feet up on the coffee table without removing footwear except in the worst snowy weather.

She often got home late and missed dad nodding off at his chair. In the morning, she'd sleep late and miss mum too, hollering half naked that she had to be out in five minutes. Except James usually had first period spare and mum would still be slipping into her wool skirt. When the house was quiet again, you'd eventually smell the black coffee and bacon dad prepared for breakfast with some leftover tomatoes, mushrooms and garlic. This might have been enough to get Maebh out of bed depending on what time her first class was and what book she had at hand.

At 3 a.m., however, she'd settle into the house quietly. She'd head straight to the fridge to nibble away at whatever was in dad's precious copper pan which was always lying there without any cover or plastic wrap and still seemed to fill the room with all the aroma that went into its preparation. She loved it best when he cooked some kind of fowl with wine and a fruit sauce. Duck with berries or quail with green grapes. She'd eat straight from the pan where it sat in the fridge without plate or cutlery, pulling pieces of meat from the bone, making sure to drown each morsel with as much congealed sauce as possible. The stuff at the bottom of the pan had most flavour and she'd scoop it up without soiling her fingers too much or upsetting the composition of food in the pan. She didn't indulge—she ate for pleasure and stopped when she was no longer transported by it.

Sitting on the couch-bed in Prague, the voyeur in her was in its own way with the family now, and imagined them laughing at the table. Everyone there, even Roisin, who is at private school in Ireland and Sinead, who left school at fourteen and is now working in the film industry. Dad would say terrifying things about the world, mum might break into song, Sinead talked budgets and Roisin and James teased each other in North Dublin accents. No one asked a single question of another—you said what you had to quickly and well, or you shut up.

There were books at home too. One, two, three billion thoughts wrapped up in publishers' seal. Books to take you somewhere near the heart of things and you read or non-read for illuminations. She could feel her eyes on them. Books radiate and you absorb what you will and the page is pleasure to the stubborn veils in a mind that bursts with pretensions. They say words begin all things but there is an inkling before that which asserts itself with a wordlessness.

She has little idea how to share with anyone. Perhaps this inkling needs no sharing where it lies inherent in the brain's grey matter.

As a child, she had made poems out of the titles, afraid to open some of the books as they could bring an end to innocence. The book of erotic art her father brought home from Japan for her mother, Yeats's *Wild Swans at Coole*, Desmond Morris's *The Naked Ape*. There might be a poem now but she can't reach for a pen. She leaves it—half formed and precious, mesmerized by itself, flickering in and out of shape.

She picks up Dante and reads the first page again, her eyes often but not always on the words she loves like a lover you turn away from to behold. She reads the Italian too enjoying it even more when she can't understand. The first line keeps resonating in fragments. "A shaded forest." "Half of my life's way." She seeks from the pages the state they put her in—meditative, drunk, ecstatic. There's an Italian textbook too. But she never gets past *essere*. She copies out the verbs but basic grammar is not something she can just hold in a haze. She never learns more than *dobrý den* and *•ěkuji* in Czech either. She had determined that this time alone away from more day to day responsibilities would get her to finally devote herself to the luxury of these pursuits. She does scribble stuff in the notepads but they might as well be empty. She is empty too. No her head holds stringing lines back and forth in the cotton baton twine. These sensations are always there but her mind seems to be in want of some kind of action so she has spent many more hours wandering the streets nursing them than sitting with them before her. There is something she needs but cannot make manifest. A vague prison round her has her stifled because she is happy enough within those walls.

The Prague minutes wade in way past when the yellow streetlights turn on and she falls asleep. She leaves the heavy night curtains open. Her whimsy might otherwise be entombed and she is expecting something.

2

She meets him, this man she is to marry, at the Canada Day party. Dubi, red curls and tie-dyed, brings him by with a gaggle of other inebriates he met about town for a party. Nationalism is everywhere and not something she is a fan of but a party is a party. In Romania, a dictator was shot but here the playwright Václav Havel has been elected President. Prague is finding itself and visitors feel the same happening to them here. He, Jean-Christophe or JC is his name, walks coltish through the faded decadence of the city on a sidewalk that rises and falls. His arms sweep wide, cradling space he likes to ignore. Framed in the dark soot stone arches, he sways—as if without bones, as if he's given them away. And while his nose is banged slightly to the left and his lips set carefully over dark stained teeth, he has elan.

"*Bonsoir,*" he says with that accent and bows theatrically, as does Maebh, in tribute.

"JC's a painter from Paris," Dubi says. Those words take her. The air glistens like honey and the ground parts way with her feet. He leads her into the event, modern silvers and the lighting too bright. The crowd welcomes them at the bar and pushes them in closer.

"Careful Maebh," says Dubi. And then he's off as she wavers between gift and warning.

"Maebh?" says JC. "How do you spell that?"

"You don't want to know," she laughs.

"What?"

"There's a 'b' and an 'h'."

"Oh!"

"But it sounds a bit like—may eve."

"*Mais* Eve, is that your name? You can call me *Mais* Adam," he says all chuffed with himself. She blushes like the wine he gives her. "Can we dance?" he says pulling her to the floor.

"I'm not sure I can dance jazz," she says and watches as he moves his hips backwards and forwards without a hint of constraint, his left arm with the cigarette brushing the air above him and his face wide open to the trance clouds of smoke.

"It's Duke Ellington—'Portrait of Wellman Braud,'" he says. "We have to dance."

"Never heard of it," Maebh says.

The trumpet is moving in so many directions—Doom, doom, doom, doom, Doom, doom—her feet clamp up with her eyes far into themselves. Jazz demands a concentration beyond what her body can translate and all the framed glass makes her feel like a photograph.

"Your back is so stiff," he says. "You aren't very good!"

"It's true," she says, too embarrassed to tell him how seriously she had studied ballet or how impressed she is he knows this music and then Dubi comes back cradling shot glasses.

"It's a vodka bar," he says. "Whatever are you doing drinking wine?" He hands the vodka to JC who has already finished his wine and takes the wine Maebh has barely touched from her hands. "Throw it back," he says handing her the tiny glass. JC is already smiling from the effects of his.

"Ouch, that's cold," she says.

"It's better than heroin," Dubi winks. "And no trace." He points to the barely discernible track marks on his arm.

"Your dad will be happy," says Maebh.

"Nah!" he grins and rushes off.

"How do you know Dubi?" JC asks.

"He's a friend from university and we came over together with Education for Democracy to teach English."

"That's a very Protestant-sounding title," he says.

"Yes, but I haven't been very useful," she says. "Most of the time, they come to class out of curiosity."

"Because you're so cute!" He takes her hands, laughing, and twirls her—like a plank of wood with holes in the middle, swooning despite itself.

And too early, just when the too-cool hues blur self consciousness into crushed lines, he loses interest and takes her back to the bar. He shifts about awkwardly in expectation and then fumbles in his pockets pulling out coins, tiny notebooks and dull pencil ends swaying all the while, that cigarette sucked into one corner of his mouth. It is a very practised gesture as if the bills should have been there but aren't and it works. Maebh understands what he wants and from then on pays for drinks as if it is nothing at all and it isn't. Everything is cheap in Prague.

She picks up the notebooks he has laid out for her perusal. The corners of the pages are scrunched over and closed tightly but somehow waiting to be turned. They are filled with drawings and scribblings and postcards of his paintings.

"This one is in New York," he says.

"Do you live there?"

"A bit. I had an exhibition there. Here I took the American flag of Jasper Johns and put this ruffled piece like this. They're from plastic coffee tops. I bent them like teeth. *Les Américains, ils bouffent le monde.*"

"What?"

"They eat the world."

The party spills out onto the street and Dubi who always appears at random times comes back and wraps his arms around them.

"Very Brit Boy," Maebh says pointing to his Oxford type platform shoes.

"We are going to an after-hours club," he says squeezing her shoulder and then he waves his arm in every direction to flag down all the cabs in Prague or people with cars pretending to be cabs.

They roll out into the crowd of tourists littering the streets with money and awe for the history rising up off every building.

"You two get in that one," Dubi says pointing to the light blue Skoda. Maebh loves how he takes charge and leads her by the hand as he ushers the others to another vehicle and shuts her in with JC alone so they can have privacy.

"You guys get into that one and who's coming with me," asks Dubi and then he barks out that we should follow him before getting into the vehicle just ahead with three others and they all head off.

They drive through the city and JC puts his hand on her leg or maybe it falls there so she looks away—the music on every corner a starry wallpaper of possibility. Time has stopped. There are Beatnik Mozart quartets, guitarists dressed like Che Guevara, a trumpeter in fedora hunched but uplifted to the moon.

JC and Maebh become separated from the rest so the taxi takes them to a spot with X-rated videos of women cutting up cantaloupe and watermelon—their breasts hang down almost touching them—but the few old world types there aren't paying any attention. Naked women are tacked up with pride in bars everywhere as a kind of tribute to emancipation.

"The way women are dressed seems to reveal so much about the political state of a country," Maebh says. "Some revolutions deck us out in veils but Prague has just opened up like Venus rising on her shell." JC tilts his head staring through the baggy shirt Maebh has tied at the waist over a long gypsy skirt.

"You are very Botticelli," he says, "but don't ruin things with your feminism."

He lights a cigarette with the detached permanence of an addict which makes it and the dangling chain of ash that hangs down from it a permanent part of him. He clings to it a bit tighter before leaning his head on the chair top by hers, just a testing second, before the fateful kiss in the garish blue strip club light.

"Tomorrow, we will go to the little house in the country where I'm staying," he says, "but tonight I'm staying with you." He hasn't left her side all evening and it is so permanent, the way he says it. Aspirations are filled in by the thin arms cradling his drink and when he turns to order another, her eyes take in the soft skin between the end of his hairline and the top of his shirt. His conversation covers so comfortably a variety of subjects crossed over into each other. Maebh's father would never bum a drink but she should have sensed the familiarity.

They take another taxi to her apartment and he undresses her. "*Tu es belle,*" he says just before passing out.

—

Maebh is in the garden in the house JC is staying at outside Prague, shielded in the filtered light she favours. The overgrown bushes and flowers shelter and the heat melts thought so the poems aren't forthcoming. JC brings her over a glass of rose. She feels his battered up Giacometti form over her and reaches for a kiss admiring how he wears chinos and white tennis shoes with the edge of a punk rocker.

"Every five minutes," he says, "you need a kiss and a cuddle" but he does seem to like it, not that he ever leans over to give her one of his own accord.

She is beginning to understand his moods. Mornings are silent. He picks himself up like she's not even there and comes back with coffee and toast in either hand. The first day when she asked him to make her some, he grumbled so much she never asks again. He reads whatever is lying around for hours and then when he eventually gets up to paint he switches to wine.

His discussions on his painting seem over-orchestrated to her. "Why don't you just paint what's out there?" she says waving her arms at the outline of town in the fields.

"*Pfouf! Ce n'est pas original*—you have to have an idea," he says.

And her, "Shakespeare and the Beatles copied" brings nothing but contempt. These days JC is studying *Le camouflage.*

"Camouflage has changed everything," he says, trying to explain the watercolours of grey stones he is working on. "You see—the English ... *les rosbifs*—they used to wear red jackets and the froggys wore blue and then they sounded the horns and marched off to die. *C'était magnifique*!"

"For the generals watching from the hills, you mean."

"But how stupid to die like imbeciles," he cries. "Then, they discovered camouflage as a way to hide in nature and Adam and Eve wore camouflage as well to hide their nudity. Today the fight is in the city." He is getting excited: "Man is alone in the city—

exposed—so it has been necessary to invent a new camouflage. A camouflage of stones."

It is brilliant, she thinks, her mind racing. Adam and Eve the first camouflage soldiers hiding in the Garden of Eden, archetypes for all men and women and the beginning of religious warfare traced back to its origins. JC was hilariously passionate about it but the studies—pages and pages of stones—she didn't see where he was going with them.

She looks at the heavy flowers and their long faded stalks furled crinkly with heat. It is lovely as the sun breezes in between the leaves. She hasn't moved from the spot in hours and only reads snippets here and there from her book.

"Why are you reading *Ulysses*?" asks JC.

"Czechoslovakia seems the perfect place to tackle it, lost as it is between old and new, East and West, poverty and wealth," she says almost to herself because JC is struggling with his ochre paint tube.

The book, however, might as well be backwards on her lap. She hears it like a melody she knows already but could never play and reads it like a book that has always been part of her having heard at home the live recordings of Joyce reading from it aloud. The famous last line is even partly why she is here—"yes yes I will Yes!" It's a cry to love really with a full heart in the rhododendrons and there is Maebh surrounded by these jaded flowers—heart aching wide but perhaps only pretending to love, she wants to so much.

"What do you mean—why am I reading it?" she says feeling all of a sudden the weight of the question but JC is back at his painting and Maebh, noticing her neglected toenails growing in all directions, tucks them and her indignation under her skirt. She has no idea where her nail clippers are and she's too happy reading what women are not supposed to be reading to realize this comes also with the fact she doesn't have enough faith in her own sex either and sees herself as better than most of them or that she's trying very hard to be better as if being a woman is not enough in itself already.

She picks up the book on Irish mythology, she's been studying at the same time, from the pile by her side. That book makes as much sense to her as *Ulysses* and she finished Kafka's *The Trial* in the same state but does feel the claustrophobia of it whenever she goes into a shop here. Buying a bathing suit seemed easy enough until she realized she hadn't seen a clothing shop anywhere. She hadn't even missed shopping as a pastime but a pale pink bikini might have been nice. Perhaps there was some government form to fill in to have one mailed out. Finally, she was led to a place that looked like it sold parts for vacuum cleaners. She stood in line for a while and then was handed an impossibly pouffy flowered thing with matching cap. The best cure for vanity, crazy lady with cane had seemed to insist as she eyed her up and—one size fits all—down. How lovely would Kafka have looked in that.

JC takes a step back to examine his painting and roll a cigarette.

"Can I have a *taffe?*" she says. Pronouncing *taffe* which means puff in French as if to dissolve herself entirely into its culture.

"Where's Mr. Leopold Bloom now," he asks, "walking the streets of Dublin behind the nice hams of a lady?" He holds his hands out as if to cup a woman's bottom. "He's my favourite character in all literature."

"He's on the strand somewhere," Maebh says.

"With the cripple?"

"I don't know." She puts down the Irish mythology and stares down at *Ulysses*—the words arched out like wings.

"*Tu es complètement nulle, tu sais*—is there anything in your head," he says passing her the cigarette in disgust. "It's not a book for women."

Maebh growls too light headed from wine and cigarettes to challenge a kind of misogyny she's grown accustomed to. Still, he's right she has no idea what's going on—strand he stands in the sand with his hand—all the sounds colliding like the petals of the universe. That's ridiculous, she laughs at the flurry of butterfly pages too unfathomable yet for traditional story speak. She reaches over for matches and lights the rollie which has gone out and puffs it again.

"Sandle-footed sunshine," she says, remembering the expression jump off the page, "that's me." But JC has stopped listening. There she is smoking at twenty-three—she thinks— having somehow managed to come off cool enough through both high school and university without succumbing. These paper thin rollies are somehow more attractive and less aggressive sticking out of your mouth and the tobacco wetter and softer. She's completely stoned after a few puffs which is how the hedonist in her likes it, so she rarely has more than that a day.

She thinks again about JC's Adam and Eve in their garden, remembering the time Dubi had dragged her off to the nude watering hole outside Prague. All the wild grasses and jangly body parts—Dubi lolling about. They had chatted about how much they admired their fathers and how little they were admired back. It was nice to have that in common and she had tried to pry him a bit further.

"What's heroin like?" she had asked him.

"Being in love."

"Ah!" she had said. "I know that addiction."

"Lucky you," he had said.

"Fake it till you make it."

And then when she had wanted the conversation to delve into these things he had run his fingers through the grass just in front of him but stared stony ahead. She had felt him pull away but then he had laughed and flopped his face down into his hands.

"Do you like my body," he had fake pouted but with a genuine need to hear so.

"Yeah! You have a nice back."

"Really! What else?"

"Auch Dubi don't turn over! I'm trying not to look at *that* if you please. I mean you have one which should be enough as far as Freud is concerned."

Maebh had leant back dying to put some clothes on but enjoying the heat of the sun. She had no idea what Dubi hoped to find. The crowd she was trying to pretend was not there seemed very heterosexual, even asexual, to her.

But Dubi had turned serious again—"I'm done with the Village People and hiding behind costumes like being gay is artifice. I need an organic scene like this in my play, natural but seductive—a gay nude watering hole heroin love scene."

He leans back in satisfaction, deliberately turning the faint track lines on his inner arms to the sun.

"Are you wearing your little girl panties again," JC says bringing her back as he comes over to get his cigarette.

It is not like she doesn't dream of silky things but simply that going out to purchase them hasn't seemed a priority. Thinking about wearing them was often enough anyway. Paradise exists, she thinks, mostly in fragments like the one JC and she are currently experiencing, but paradise is also something you invent. She thinks of Adam and Eve again, with leaves camouflaging their nakedness and the irony of how a naked human body, however much the nudists might disagree, rather clashes with nature. It is always presented as though Adam and Eve cover up their distinctive sexuality in shame but perhaps it is more to blend in better with the world around them and that the one thing that distinguishes humans from the animal world is how fragile nudity is. Clothing, Maebh thinks, is something which might protect men and women not just from nature but the god-type eyes they might have felt afraid of. Covering up might then have heightened their desperate lusts and undressing have served as a kind of symbolic trust they had in each other—an unveiling of self to other—not just physically but metaphysically as well.

Maebh wishes she could speak to JC about her wandering thoughts but then she couldn't put them in writing either or even remember where the argument started. The concerns are so huge and impossible to decipher. The great veil of clothing, a form of protection from the elements that somehow through time became ritualized. Removing it is an act of faith and vulnerability that could not be felt if not worn in the first place.

Her pen is so heavy she could never lift it now. The gentle wind sneaks in through the garden and it's as if it takes every thought with it. The wine and cigarettes, flights of bees and that fading flower smell have done her in, and then she could never do those sensations justice. An actual word on the tongue or page might even be a violation of the experience of thought.

Maebh listens to JC go on with a little cackle about that bitch Eve driving humanity out of Eden with her lust. She wonders, enjoying her own creative paralysis and how she is letting her passions lead her towards unexplainable life choices, if Eve hadn't moved in a similar state towards that apple and with one arbitrary bite instead done us all a favour. A symbol of temptation and our essential curiosity, we are, Maebh thinks, a banal lot without her. Has she sold her soul with this acceptance or merely decided that no matter how much she hates social injustice and how hard she might try to live well, she is sure that suffering must prevail.

JC is mumbling things out of the fridge for dinner—"the carrots are flaccid like my penis," he says.

Maebh extricates herself from her spot to hug and help out. He says these things, she thinks, losing herself now in the skin of his neck which is always much warmer than hers, to make her laugh and she does. He doesn't really come off vulgar either but as one nonchalantly challenging bourgeois pruderies. And Maebh seems determined to enjoy this aspect of him. They are having fun but being young in Prague accounts for a large part of that. Much affection is there—they cook, eat and walk everywhere together and have lots to talk about just as it had been two summers ago in Munich with Maxim. She had had her first orgasm ever, alone or with a man, at twenty-one years of age and then for the rest of the summer three times a day till it was over. But she hasn't had one since. Between the sheets with JC, it wasn't working as well. Perhaps he wasn't that enamoured with her body or perhaps the desire wasn't there.

"Look at that ass," he says. "It doesn't matter that those tits are so small."

It had taken some time with Maxim to get to that point where they were no longer self-conscious body parts in a bed together. She had found a way to move but more that there was an overwhelming sense of trust and then it was as if he carried her everywhere in a state of bliss. She had even had that Boucher poster of Eros and Psyche framed to put over the bed. This lasted till he had looked down on her as if she had gone too far, as if the sight of her pleasure disgusted him or interfered with his own. At first, he had been pleased, proud of himself but then it was as if he preferred her staid. It was as if looking at her he saw her need and then inevitably his own too which broke the magic of it and sullied things.

And then there had been the unplanned for pregnancy that had seemed to come as punishment. It was as if nature preferred her staid as well.

3

She is twenty-one an• with Maxim in Munich. They have come here for the summer to live that life. She will go back to get her •egree but Maxim is •one with all that. If he ha• a •egree, he woul• throw it in the air.

He has oranges and takes her by the hand. It's like being a child again. He walks her to a spot under the trees where the sun shines in just so and spreads the oranges out on the same brown paper they were wrapped in.

There were some strawberries in season but Maxim only eats one thing at a time. He cuts his orange with the knife they bought at the army surplus store on Yonge street. It has a well-shaped bone handle and a sharp blade that fol•s into it.

Everything is a ritual and he carves through the skin making one long smooth coile• rin• before he breaks the insi•e up into sections. Then he watches with disdain as she claws through hers, spurting juice and wiping her jeans with the residue.

He becomes the reveren• of foo• libations. She lets him fee• her an• oranges never tasted so good.

They are learning Ancient Greek and pull out books to copy conjugations. Hers such a mess of scratchings she looks over at his scrolle• in a balance of curls an• space.

She is not going to be able to get very far with his strategies because he insists on perfecting a verb, a form, a letter before moving on. Legibility and she are at odds and memorizing has no part in her ad hoc *world.*

She looks away to a•mire the sky an• the soun• of the fountain an• to contemplate the overall peace. Then she puts her pencil to notebook to write a line about oranges but he is focuse•, bent over till he lifts his hea• when it's time to go back to the library.

They cling to each other an• their books rising from their painting an• people coo over them. They move forwar• but he must be carrying her—long hair slicke• to her face an• feet away from the groun•.

The library is a dark cool cavern with high arched moldings twisted in gol•. There are rows of books in cases with etche• glass •oors, tiny wrought iron knobs an• coloure• figures in every win•ow. It coul• be a church an• they sit, heads bent in whispers.

He has Frazer's The Golden Bough. *All eleven volumes photocopied in tiny font an• he sits squinting. She has Robert Graves's* The Greek Myths *like a brick in her bag and she wonders about all the words dedicated to the workings of male sacrifice, the traces of matrilineal societies an• the grapplings of early history with what it meant to be alive .*

They have nearly finishe• their books, plumpe• up as if every book has been written into their system and with all they learn about myth, traced in religion, trace• in war, trace• in fear.

They should have been learning German though she thinks. Maxim's mother is German and so is the uncle who lent them the studio but Maxim wants to start at the beginning to scoop the basin of civilization out from Gilgamesh to Ovid to Goethe.

Love raises an intuition of all things or their love •i•. An• being in love raise• timeless was the best state, in fact, to un•erstan• the mysterious movements of man through the history these books uncovere•.

European parents are something they have in common. The only •ifference is that Maebh's go back to Ireland whenever possible but Maxim's mum has never returned to Germany nor has she taught her son German.

And they both have European passports but Maxim would never work there or anywhere. His mother, who owns a small deli, sends him money every month. Maebh, though, will have to work at some point. Her parents make much more but she's been on her own financially since the university she pai• for herself, too prou• even to ask for loans an• lazy with the paperwork it would have taken to get them.

She feels, in fact, that she must pay for things, so she too often pai• for him.

Maebh and Maxim continue on through parks and gardens with Sappho an• Homer in their han•s sharing meals at fountains. Munichen means by the monks place so they stu•y like monks at the shrine of love.

An• it is here after a few weeks an• thereafter for some months three times a •ay that she lays her hea• back on the square white pillows. Maxim puts his penis insi•e her but somehow it's •ifferent an• she feels great pleasure and heat inside her and up her body. Maxim stops still in wonder above her while she moves her hips and pulls them up as tight against him as she can. An• then she feels such joy an• softness that she laughs an• laughs in •isbelief.

Not that an orgasm is so extraor•inary for two lovers in a foreign lan• with colours too bright and pine wood walls except that she had never had one. Not with other men before this an• not on her own or by acci•ent with a showerhead somehow.

4

A priest JC met in a bar lent him the country house for a month as long as JC gave him a place to stay in Paris when he next visited. JC laughs a kind of cruel silly laugh about it which Maebh doesn't understand means that the said generous Czech will be spending the night on some bench at the Gare du Nord. She does understand that JC's month is up and that although it isn't properly discussed and they haven't been together long, he is now living with her.

"You have nowhere else to stay," she asks.

"Not until my money arrives," he says.

He is waiting for a wire of funds from France and now she is paying for their food as well as their drink. Things don't cost much and feeling alive is worth the expense, she reasons though she might have become a kind of reverse Faustus paying for a soul, or love, or the artist's life as she did before with Maxim when it was already hers for free.

People come and go. Dubi disappeared again. "Where the hell is Dubi? I can't live without him," she says. And then she forgets he even exists.

They meet people everyday on the streets: two conductors in training from Vienna, a guy from Alberta, a Czech girl with long brown legs. They all go to a bar and drink shot glasses of freezing cold vodka so fresh it shocks the throat. A well-dressed fellow comes by selling caviar in a rucksack. One of the conductors buys some—it's the black expensive kind—and they pass it around the table eating it straight from the jar with spoons. They need real food soon, however, and JC offers to prepare a *poulet basquaise* at their apartment, or hers, or Frantisek's grandmother's apartment to be exact but who knows who is who or what these days.

"We have a few tomatoes but just need white wine," JC says. So they pick some up and pile into taxis. Maebh snuggles into JC's shoulder—the last of the sunset bursting across the windshield and the bleakness of the grey apartment towers radiating their usual pink evening permanence within the crumblings of communism.

"How much do you pay for your place?" asks the guy from Alberta.

"Nothing," says Maebh.

"Who d'you sleep with?"

"Ahm! A few guys," she blushes. "But no the company I teach at were very appreciative of my coming here to help them. I feel guilty about it because I love travel more than I believe learning to speak English will save anyone."

"You mean you aren't an angel."

"You look like one," says Conductor B.

"Riiight!" says Alberta.

Maebh blushes again and passes around some wine while JC heads to the kitchen with the other bottles. He is a really good cook and he sweeps up too and so afraid is Maebh of being the wife trudge that this is more important to her than any money he might contribute to the relationship.

Conductor A puts on a cassette and starts lecturing about a certain Baroque composer who "broke through the boundaries of conformity" or some such thing.

"What's the deal with conformity?" Maebh asks.

"Conformity, my dear, is when you say yes because you cannot say no."

"But maybe," she says, "you just want to fit in. There's a kind of harmony in that."

"Maebh can you chop the onions," says JC. He starts going on about "*le jus*" and "*les sauces*" and dry American palettes. "Ah, they don't even know what a shallot is." He stands there, cigarette hanging out of the left side of his mouth, pouring wine into the pan for an eternity while the delicious steam billows all around. He keeps staring at Czech girl with that head down but looking up with furrowed brow thing. It is like having a really French Johnny Depp in your kitchen.

"Are these your drawings?" asks Czech girl, pointing to the papers of stone and camouflage hanging from the wall. "I wanted to paint too," she says, "but the government put me in accounting. You are lucky you have freedom in the West."

Maebh sympathizes with her but is wary of the euphoric idealization of Western democracy taking hold in Eastern Europe. Not that she hadn't herself idealized communism before coming here—seeing it as a system that never had a proper chance to evolve.

"Freedom comes with people sleeping on the street," Alberta says. Maebh nods in agreement, loving the sense of security that oozes off the fact that everyone seems to have been guided into a job and an apartment here while accepting that she would have had a hard time living within a system that seems to have led to a kind of conformity or stagnation.

"Are you able to paint in the evenings or on weekends," Maebh asks Czech girl.

"Yes!" she says and seems ready to expound on this till JC cuts her off with a laugh.

"You either paint or you don't," he says. "It's not a sideline."

"That's easy enough," Maebh says but probably not out loud, "when someone else is paying the bills." But this doesn't mean she is less awed by JC's confidence in his status as an artist to step away from the breadwinner role she has too easily stepped into.

"Do you make a living as an artist?" says Conductor A.

"*Non*!" says JC, "but the graphic designers do."

Conductor B spits out his drink with laughter and so does Maebh proud of how easily he brings down the assumption that you are not a real artist unless you are doing it for a living. But Maebh has other theories of her own.

"Art is dead," she says. "It has attached itself to the worst kind of religiosity. Artists are as revered as priests once were and go about it with a tad too much reverence and self-importance".

"Speak for yourself," says JC.

And as is often the case Maebh wonders if she isn't talking shite. Everyone is now off in little corners onto other subjects and Czech girl has taken off the baroque and is now dancing to ABBA.

"*Elle est magnifique,*" JC says. "I want to run my hands all the way up her legs."

Maebh continues hacking at the onions, tears starting to flow.

"The gas is off again! I can smell it," she says diverting her glance to the stove top.

"I've got it," says conductor B. He pulls out a match for the stove with a little bang and then lights a cigar.

"I wanna try," she says. He comes really close and shows her how to drag from it. "Aughghgh."

JC starts chopping up the chicken. "I will destroy this bird!"

"That knife is bigger than you, JC."

Conductor B moves away and Maebh follows him. "Is this what you are reading?" he says picking up *Ulysees.* "What's it like?"

"It's like Beethoven's 'Emperor' Concerto, *Rhapso•y In Blue* and The Pogues all in one," she says looking at their cassettes on the floor.

"Glenn Gould," says Conductor A looking through them, "That Stokowski recording is unique but when will you Canadians get over your obsession with your Mr. Gould."

"At least I don't dress like him," she says pointing to Conductor B wrapped up in scarves and gloves.

"I'm cold always," and then he whispers in her ear,"I don't have you to keep me warm."

"Who else would they worship other than Oscar Peterson," says JC.

"Heh!" says Alberta. "We have Neil Young, Leonard Cohen—way cooler than what you Frenchies call music these days."

JC goes back to the kitchen mumbling something about how they have obviously never heard of Serge Gainsbourg.

"This cassette says 'Back'. Can't you spell over there?" says Conductor A.

"It's a great typo don't you think?"

"Gustav Holst," says Conductor A still perusing through the tapes. "Which one?"

"Holst is garbage," JC says coming out of the kitchen brandishing two nearly empty bottles over his head.

"Jupiter," she says.

"The God of all the planets—noble and glorious that Jupiter not like the Greeks and their Zeus."

"Don't insult the Greeks," says JC.

"Zeus is nothing but a pervert."

"*Et alors*! At least, he makes you laugh."

Conductor B puts on The Pogues.

"My *grand-grand-père* was Greek and in the *Aca•émie française*."

"And what shit did he write?" says Conductor A.

"I'll kill you too like the chicken."

"JC did you finish all that wine?" Maebh asks.

"No, I put it in the chicken."

"Two whole bottles?"

"I'll go get more," he says trying to encourage Czech girl to keep dancing.

Then he trips over the armchair and squeals from the floor.

The song "Waltzing Matilda" comes on and JC sings about lost arms and legs. He gets up swaying and bouncing like the walls are moving but falls crashing down again. His tiny dark eyes floating helpless in his head. "Maebh help me!"

She is suddenly, though drunk, far too calm. "Everything is closed JC. We've had enough to drink."

"*Non, j'y vais*!" but he can't move this time.

"What's that smell?" asks Czech girl."

"*Du feu*!"

"The chicken is burning," says Alberta.

"I'll get it," says Conductor B. He turns off the stove and puts the pot, thick smoke wafting from it, on the balcony, and opens all the windows.

"Let's get out of here," says Czech girl choking.

"Come," says Conductor B. He pulls Maebh gently by the dress and a spark goes just as gently through her. She sees their life—Vienna, his capable hands and long soft eyelashes.

"I don't know how."

"You can't stay here!" He is right but that's not how it feels.

"The smoke is terrible," says Conductor A. "I'm leaving. She doesn't want you my friend."

"Stay! Stay!" but not loud enough and Maebh kneels down to remove JC's shoes, knowing full well that it's not the first or the last time she will let the right man get away.

"I want wine," says JC. Maebh walks over to the sink and lays an elbow on the counter. "*Waltzing Matilda*" is still playing. She drinks as much water as she can too quickly and then vomits.

"Maebh, Maebh, where are you?"

Maebh opens the cupboard under the sink looking for a rag. There are hundreds, maybe thousands of plastic bags folded up perfectly into tiny butterflies in a large shopping bag. She could throw them out the window, let them fly for a moment and then watch them slowly drift to the ground.

JC is singing but Maebh needs quiet and walks over to him lying there. He shushes and pulls her down to curl round like a crescent moon. His eyes empty as coal.

—

After one of the rare mornings they spend apart, JC meets Maebh at the park, past where the creaky trams traverse the slopes by the candy castle that now houses the Czechoslovakian government. Sculpted grapes cascade the walls and the peacock strolls fluttering tail and poésie. JC has two roses in his hands.

"The red one is me," he says, "and the pink one is you."

It's so precious she doesn't notice that the red rose is closed in perfectly and the pink falling loosely with arms blighted to any sense of self.

"My money hasn't arrived yet so my mother can't make the transfer."

She doesn't even ask what money. He has come off like it grows on trees and that's what he lets her believe. This means that she will never get what she 'lent' him but this doesn't interfere with the roses. Disappointment shrugs off in the warm bliss airs.

"I have to go back to Paris but you could come with me?"

"Okay!" she says.

"Or you could marry me?"

His head—beauty on the cusp of decay—turns away. She thinks of Antonin Artaud pre-asylum when she sees him and with maybe too much pity. JC doesn't kneel or anything when he asks her because they are walking arm in arm. He does say it like it means something to him though but not anything about what she means to him or what they will do together. He doesn't give her a ring either because then she's hiding her face in his shoulder.

"So?" and maybe he seems to hold his breath here.

"Of course!" she says. "Yes!" because she's thinking of Molly Bloom again and her love lofty by the sea which Bloom is more worthy of, all in all, than JC.

"We will live in Paris," Maebh says, "and where the wind takes us. Lucky me, I've grown wings."

He laughs, proud even.

"You'll work there? Sell paintings?" she says in that order but without asking him how or why her or why marriage or listening to the crashing doubts. She sees what she wants to see.

They walk by the bright garden colours—hedges, grass and flowerbeds blurring like an overexposed photograph. Beauty too primary to resist.

"You forget all about Stalin here," she says.

"The main issue apart from the gulags was closing all the borders and exerting limitations on education and jobs."

Maebh squeezes his arm. With a minimum of sentences they often agree on things larger than themselves. And she sees this as sign enough to proceed. His arm holds her balanced at the edge of Europe—dank, dilapidated but feisty. She is open and her artist's life moves onward. Such is the love that she might have switched on with a flip.

Maebh can imagine life without JC and could go back to Toronto and teach. Her father had written to say he had lunched with the Dean at a college who would hire her. She could also take evening courses to upgrade and then try for grad school. But her parents are moving back to Ireland again and while she does have friends in Toronto, JC has somehow erased the past. She could also of course go to Paris by herself. But why? She has only known JC three or four months but has been with him always since then. There's a confidence she gets from this, and she feels stronger in his presence.

Mostly, she wants this exuberance to last, and so—as they head down the cobble streets by a tram to the river—she says yes to hold on to it for them. As if, through marriage, they can forever roam the pastel of these streets on a miracle of $900 in savings that has somehow made her wealthier than a doctor here.

Still, it happens too easily and quickly to be true. Why ever would they want to get married or need to so she's sure it is all talk and not bound to happen. There is no true friend to look at her in a way that would remind her of what it means to be a rational human being so she lets the fact that someone wants to spend the rest of his life with her seal itself in her mind. A fact that will get her through more than it should when the reality of all that this marriage will entail makes itself apparent. A surge of contentment sweeps loneliness into cobbled corners she'd rather deal with sometime later. It's not very feminist but she likes the idea of being married and if that idea is not what it should be, she can live on an imagined better version of it. But mostly, she wants to walk away from everything she knows, to call up within herself the breezy secrets of Bohemian Europe. And that seems easier to do with JC.

They walk across the Charles Bridge and stand there together for sometime watching the gathering of swans. More trams heading up to the castle pass on the left.

"They mate for life," says JC pointing to the swans and then he flicks his cigarette into the Vltava.

He pulls out an art magazine with Jeff Koons and Cicciolina on the cover. Kitschy everywhere. Jeff is naked and Cicciolina looks like a swan herself—white hair, corset, stockings in the air and long painted nails covering her pussy. Jeff and Cicciolina get married too and have a child but Cicciolina hardly speaks a word of English and the marriage falls apart but there's something poetic about their connection.

"The river was dammed in the 1950's and no longer runs through with waves," Maebh says quoting Frantisek. She can't stop staring at the magazine and thinks how she doesn't mind floods and wishes it had never been tamed.

"You need that orgasm though first," says JC rifling through the pages without any sense of *pudicité*. Jeff and his porn star frame their explicit infatuation in innocence. "You can't have marriage without an orgasm."

At least it looks like Jeff and Cicciolina have that, Maebh thinks.

They might be having three or four conversations—not one as important as it should be but touched he noticed Maebh coos little things in his ear. "I'll have many many orgasms. It will just take more time."

JC usually prefers the working class bars but they head over to Café Slavia where they are supposed to meet Dubi and they find him, like every other tourist *comme intellectuel,* slouched over one of Václav Havel's plays.

"Duuubi! Where have you been," Maebh says and he gives her that look implying a whole world of things a gay man is privy to. She hugs him tight round his full chest and wonders what it might be like to dress up as a man in his world.

JC orders cakes and his cigarette bends within the grand window frames while Dubi tells them about the play he hopes to write.

"I want you to be in it Maebh," he says.

"No, no those days are over."

JC laughs. "Why would you put her in it?"

"Actually, Maebh has done quite a few plays and was even the lead in a short film," Dubi says.

"Bah! You were a dancer and an actress—and played piano too—like all the good girls?" says JC a bit proud despite the mocking and then he continues on with Dubi about the play.

Maebh pretends not to notice this or some of the film students from Dubrovnik she used to meet up with. They don't wave either as she had dated one for a spell. He had taken a few photos of her kneeling between the nylon drapes at his window, removed his Charlie Chaplin attire and laid himself out as if at his wake. She had given him a blowjob because he asked for it and she had never given one before. She had put his penis in her mouth with indifference. His flesh clammy, wanting sunlight. She had sensed in his body some duty to him, the pain of old world Europe—soldiers rolling through stone, great books written and torn, lines redrawn, people cowering in mud hills and all the haunting darknesses so she gave herself to him for that.

"You can be my geisha girl," he had said as she let the sperm drool out the side of her mouth onto the bedding relieved it had not gone on too long.

A few years ago, a sweet guy had insisted on going down on her once and she'd felt an odd nothing then as well.

"Wakey, wakey Maebh," JC says.

"Look at you blushing," says Dubi.

Maebh wipes her forehead and comes back to the room.

"I was just telling JC about the time we snuck into the President's box during Smetana's the *Bartered Bride* at the Opera House," Dubi says.

"I wish Havel still hung out here," Maebh says looking past the plush chairs of Café Slavia as if they miss something.

"An usher came to tell us," Dubi says, "and Maebh had squealed—'Havel sits here?'

"Ha!" Maebh says "but Dubi was after the red cheeked country boy usher."

"Maebh," says Dubi, "you look like you are sitting on Havel's lap right now?"

"Oh! I almost forgot. JC asked me to marry him," she says.

This somehow seems more accurate than all she was thinking and suddenly she understands that she might be marrying him to answer the many questions she hasn't even properly formulated. And then she is afraid she has signed herself up for civility instead of this quest and various abandons. But Dubi stands up—hair in all directions and a touch regretful the blatant comforts of marriage are denied him—to grab her. She pulls JC into their hug. Warmth all round. Dubi, choking up a bit, reaches all of a sudden into his knapsack. He pulls out a wad of *koruna* and then they are off to a restaurant with the best smoked salmon in town.

Maebh is unaccustomed to such generosity and Dubi is usually careful with his money but JC attracts such gestures with the air of genius he gives off. As they are seated in an elegant room, Maebh remembers how rich Dubi is and the whispers round campus of his sex paying habits. And how in a desperate state for that or maybe it was for heroin, he had sold her a Sony Walkman that had never worked and how after she hadn't spoken to him for months.

The food smells better than anything here since her Czech students had invited her into their homes. They have rare pieces of beef you would never find anywhere else in the city.

"Ah! les Belges!" JC says, referring to the large table next to them speaking French and then whispers a joke at their expense. *Les Belges* it turns out are the Paddies and/or Newfies of the Francophone world.

JC orders the most *parfait* wine he has drunk since Paris and the Franglais they've been speaking all summer becomes more convoluted. *Les Belges* seem a bit curious about them and start speaking to JC in French. He informs them that Maebh is Irish and a lovely singer neither of which is completely true and then; and this is out of character because Maebh is normally shy about these things, they have her singing a sad Irish song with her choir voice which really needed a whole choir to be heard. Still, they like it and ask for another so she gives them Yeats's "Down By the Sally Garden" but the waiters beg her to sit down as graciously as they can which is too bad because she's just getting started. Her voice has become noticeably less choir like as she starts on "I've been a wild rover" so she does sit but too many drinks have been consumed and JC and Dubi are now singing "La Marseillaise."

Things move fast in that slow way and they are given the bill without desserts and their table is stripped bare. The maître d' then leads them out of the restaurant with the decorum reserved for nobility. At the next table, JC informs—as they head off in fits to their favourite wine bar—were the Belgian Ambassador to Czechoslovakia and his entourage. JC pulls up to a tree with Maebh on his arm to hold them steady and Dubi immortalizes the night with his camera. There they are, a darkly drunk poetic type willowed ecstatic round a young woman—too rosy and starry eyed to notice.

Maebh goes back often to the photo and to where they had nestled on the Charles Bridge to blame her ambivalence on its quarrel with the flattened river, the four or five swans and Cicciolina with her red mouth. Each side of the city had taken its stand: the mysterious old town streets and the eighteenth-century purple castle. She could not reconcile herself any which way to what life is or who she was. Her mind dallied in the wind. You could somehow even in the triumph that resonated all over Prague sense greater difficulties for the region and for her. No Prague might fare better than she. Was it even ambivalence that carried her forth? Or a desire to step out of the hiding she had been in since childhood? She didn't know where one could draw lines on these maps or define a plan of action. She must have known not to marry JC but all the same it felt the right thing to do. She could just have given thanks for the wildest summer of her life and found a way to Paris on her own, except an easier path there had positioned itself in front of her.

Was she herself the placid river—the geographic wrapped up confusion? The stilled current ran from her sandals to the sun in her hair—too sweet for caution and too ignorant. She saw her dissolution softening through its reflection on the river. Some twenty years of life and books and she was nothing. The blank canvas speckled with shadows. Shadows that had slipped through the cracks any sense of practicality held together before this semblance of a love affair. She flew into the arms of a man who might not even see her. He was, however, always there and hers and that is a feeling she had never known and she was more determined than she realized to step forth in the experiment of life to feel something more than nothing—to feel it all.

5

Upon their return from Munich, Maxine an• Maebh watch anxiously every month for it to arrive. She never knows exactly when. They are so happy when it •oes an• it is in the flow of bloo• that they feel most alive.

Except even as they manage some days to make their way to lectures, she •oes get pregnant, which is fine, birth control is the biggest threat to human happiness, con•oms •ull the sensations, the pills she forgets to take, make her •epresse• an• the cap thing with all that goo in it keeps falling off.

She tells her parents this when she writes the letter to explain the abortion. It feels light—unreal—but necessary. Why shoul• pleasure ruin your life?

They call her from Irelan• the night before the proce•ure an• keep her on the phone for hours. They will help her, says Mum. Sinea• says she is evil an• her father's gentle voice con•emns her to the asylum:

"Babies are just what you do when you love someone. That's the essential purpose of life. Those women who aban•on motherhoo• for career an• family planning lose their min•s or turn into shoul•er-pa••e• Thatcherites."

Have I gone back to the 19th century? she thinks.

But then she feels like any animal in the swoon of nature's great pull to procreate an• the part of her that moves through life as it •rags her an• does too much what she is told over what she does know is best, buys into the great unwritten Irish Catholic law that passion be permitted only with procreation.

Maxim paces in front of her—"You are •estroying my life."

If only he ha• also mentione• how she woul• be •estroying her life too an• explaine• that she woul• not be able to finish school or rea• books.Or worse still if anyone ha• thought how they woul• be •estroying the life of a child they decided to just so haphazardly birth without jobs or a house of their own. If the •octrines announce• planne• parenting as a tribute to life rather than its antithesis, she might have un•erstoo• an• come back to her senses. Having a child because you really wanted one could be that step forwar• in evolution beyon• rape an• ma• love-in big oopsies to a healthier culture.

As usual there was too much she coul• not formulate or perhaps she covete• the wrath her lack of will woul• inflict on her person. Her whole self is cra•ling a precious chil• she now pictures with Maxim's curly hair and her blue eyes.

"You will make it work," Maebh's mum says. "Everyone does."

Do they mum? Maebh thinks but she can't say it because being over-pre-pare• is never cool an• she coul•n't say it without saying, •i• our family make it work?

Maebh starts bleeding rather heavily one week later though and they go to hospital. There's no heartbeat and the room goes still.

"I took Gravol on the bus tour through the black forest before I knew I was pregnant," she says.

"No, no, it's not your fault!" they say.

She loses everything. The chil• she coul•n't have properly care• for, the respect of her parents, her semester, Maxim an• the sexual confi•ence an•

joy opene• so briefly only to close. She loses also her own sense of self-respect an• falls into •epression.

What curse is it to be a woman?

Rea•ing Ovi•'s Metamorphosis *beneath the tree by Hart House at the university an• then in the stu•y room, she toils with the primor•ial mess of all that occurre•. Love, orgasm, her own fertility, the •esire for an abortion an• the loss of the growing fetus hang over her like snake-hea• Me•usa.*

She rea•s an• rea•s of the great universal journeys. Her as yet unknown quest is to quell the lust for following life on a whim that not even this experience can amend.

6

JC meets her at Charles de Gaulle airport with Djamila, a film-maker from Cameroon, all glow with freckles, generous parents and a red Mini Cooper.

"It's a modest place," JC warns. "Apartments are almost as hard to find here as they are in Prague."

"Maybe you can stay at mine next month while I'm gone?" says Djamila in near perfect English.

"Nice tits and a nice ass too don't you think," JC says. "I'm going to put them in a painting."

Maebh is a bit jealous.

"JC we'd love you just as much if you weren't so rude." Djamila says. "All his friends have messed with me but JC always kept his hands to himself," she says putting her arm over Maebh's shoulder.

"Where did you learn your English?" Maebh asks.

"My step-father is from Pittsburg and I went to school there a few years," she says.

Maebh feels decidedly at home as she crouches her way into Djamila's Mini past a gorgeous pair of brown suede boots and a bunch of scripts. They whirl round the lanes of the *peripherique,* past tall suburbia, Roland Garros and the motorbikes passing by even faster. Car roof down—it blows by grey like purgatory.

"J'ai soif," says JC

She had been thirsty too getting off the plane but had said they couldn't buy anything when JC headed straight to the airport bar. She has $200 left to her name which will go nowhere here.

"That's it?" JC had said.

She had hoped he might have a job and some money of his own but refused to give into disappointment when he didn't.

JC had just shrugged and shouldered his way out, hands in big pockets. She is at least allowed to be almost as broke as he is. Maebh doesn't even miss the clean clean candy tones of Prague or mind having less. The buildings are dark with grit enough for clenched teeth and there's poetry in that.

JC had gone on ahead to sort things out and she had stayed in Prague to say goodbye to the company she had taught at and return the keys to the apartment. Except, she hadn't really done that. She had tried to put all the knick-knacks she had hidden in the closet back and called Frantisek only to say the keys were on the kitchen table and to get help with a taxi to the airport.

"It's been that summer," she had told him knowing he'd forgive her—"*velmi, velmi, velmi!*"

"If the taxi doesn't come let me know," he had said.

"How is Priya?" she had asked.

"She's pregnant!"

"I'm so happy for you both!"

"Thank you! She lights up my life."

"And gives you hope too, right," Maebh says but she doesn't laugh because he sounds teary.

Maebh had left a Nižbor crystal vase for them with a dried out rose and water line that Dubi had bought her beside the key with a card. It was a paltry gesture for they had been very good to her and when she had picked up her bag to leave, she had noticed that the place needed a vacuum but seemed tidy—like her life.

"Actually our apartment is a dump," JC says again as they pull up to what will be home for a few weeks until they move to Djamila's.

It's not actually an apartment but a tiny storage space with a closet sink and hole-in-the-floor loo. There are glass doors looking out over a concrete patio strewn with old plastic chairs—the whole thing is stuffed high with furniture except the bed which has sheets and a blanket and looks as if someone had tried to make it homey but is too pathetic to be bohemian even when they light some candles.

They lie about many days there, between dinner invites and nibbling on the bits JC steals at Franprix. She gives him a chance to be the money guy but then, tummy rumbling, she goes looking for work. She has done crap jobs since she was 10 and is used to having something in her pocket so she puts her pride away easily enough.

The September air is grey and heavy but she has stepped out of summer's cocoon—job, dinner, sleep—moth-like and sticky round the pantry.

She jumps the metro turnstiles like a brat but she really doesn't have the fare. The gâteau at Slavia was exquisite but, British passport in hand, she walks about the tourist spots to ask for work. She stuffs *pizza bianca* with cabbage and raisin salad, near St. Michel, while opera extracts blare onto the street, she answers calls on the telephone two afternoons a week with Richard Ellman's biograghy of James Joyce on her lap at the office of JC's mother, and she babysits for a movie star-looking couple who gives them tins of food as payment.

Those days, however, pass quickly. Djamila's place is very spacious and then a girl from Cork Maebh meets in a pub tells her what to do and say to get a job teaching at a language school called Languainc and a friend of a friend moving to La Réunion gets them to sign over the lease to their apartment in the 18th. Things fall together so well Maebh almost forgets how much JC is ignoring her while he paints every day at a studio someone found for him and how he couldn't even take one day to show her round Paris.

When she meets JC's parents, she finds out that JC never received his baccalaureate and that he had dropped out of Beaux-Arts after one year. He has also according to them never made a penny aside from a few paintings sold and welfare money and has been a complete and utter embarrassment to them their whole lives.

Odd jobs don't seem to be something the French middle-class take on, however, and most restaurants hire "real" professionals and not hip university students like they do in North America. Maebh is almost embarrassed at how her practical side pretends to a lack of higher purpose and or self and makes her feel a sideshow to JC's dedication to his status as a painter. She hates to be so plebeian but doesn't even hate the work. Fortunately, JC's parents don't seem to look down on her, perhaps because she is paying the rent and feeding the pair of them which means they don't have to.

"Why are you marrying my son," his father asks as if Maebh shouldn't be doing so and was cut of better cloth.

She likes his parents all the same. They arrive to take them out to dinner in matching navy blazers over t-shirts with graphics and blue jeans. Pierre wears soft soled loafers and Delphine white sneakers. They comment on Maebh's British table manners and how chic she looks in her tweed jacket over flowered dress.

It's the nicest restaurant she has been to in Paris. The walls are painted dark and hung with gilded mirrors and the soft leather banquets are apricot. Everything and everyone here is put-together but not over-stylized. His father translates the menu for her with the stuffiest British accent which betrays, as hoped, his gentile education.

"I know it's cliche but if you have never tried frog's legs you must try these," he says.

And when Maebh orders them, the magret canard and profiterole without hesitation, his mother laughs, *"elle est une petite gourmande!"*

"What's your favourite book", Pierre asks when he learns she went to university to get what he calls *Un Diplôme* instead of *Une Licence.*

"I don't know! *Ulysses,*" Maebh says, "even though I haven't really grasped it all".

"Not mine!" he says.

"Have you read it?" she asks.

"Twice!" he says. Maebh doesn't believe him but that shuts her up. Besides the frog's legs have arrived—slightly deep fried with fresh herbs, a bit of frisée, lemon and cream.

His favourite writers are all English—Sir Walter Scott and Somerset Maugham. He paraphrases the Maugham story about the woman who eats everything on the menu much to the consternation of her rather cash-strapped date and was surprised to hear that she was familiar with it. "So witty!" he laughs or sputters with lips closed.

Maebh doesn't laugh with him as she has all night. Delphine even wondered how she showed her teeth so freely.

And JC added, "See how she slaps her little hand on her knee."

"You don't like Maugham?" JC's father says and seems a bit hurt—"why?"

Maebh likes him a lot for noticing and having a genuine desire for an answer.

"It's snobby and unenlightened," she says.

"Bah", he says, "What does that mean?"

"*Boule •e Suif* has a more generous depiction of female appetite."

"Maupassant," he nods. "You've read that too?"

"Have you read any other French writers?" Delphine pipes in.

Maebh's face is flushing. She is enjoying the attention but wonders why people are so often surprised she reads books. She rolls off a list which includes a bit of Balzac, whose depictions of bourgeois preoccupations with manners over genuine kindness she truly is coming to appreciate in the presence of JC's parents.

They bring the main courses now. The magret comes over a salad and Maebh now wishes she had ordered the bavette but she's as happy not to overeat—a symptom of the on the cusp food disorder that afflicts so many of her sex.

"You should read Marguerite Duras," Delphine says, "*C'est très beau—L'Amant!*"

"I don't read women writers," Maebh says.

"*Oui, c'est •e la mer•e!*" JC laughs and starts on about how Philippe Sollers told Duras she wasn't fuckable on national TV. "That was even funnier than when Gainsbourg told Whitney Houston the exact opposite."

His parents find that funny too but Maebh is preoccupied now by a deep raised scar on Pierre's hand she can't stop staring at.

"I got this during the Algerian war when my jeep crashed into a wall and caught fire," he brags. The damaged hand curls like a paw—mottled moist clay—he pets it with the fingers from his other hand. "Like most of the officers, I never saw combat but went home with a medal. Look at how you disapprove," he sputters and Maebh appreciates again how observant he is for she does try to hide it.

JC chooses this time to ask his parents for money for furniture which they refuse, as they always have done to help him even a little—not that they should but because they are the controlling types who would if he lived the toe-the-line life they had set out for him.

"If you want to give up the bourgeois life for art, go right ahead but don't complain about it."

Fair enough but it seems like a kind of punishment Maebh thinks as she tries to manoeuvre as much chocolate sauce as possible onto each bite of profiterole with her knife. JC is cradling ice cream delicately in his left cheek cavity as far away from his poor teeth as possible. She knows his parents have not gotten where they have with greater self-reliance. His father had scrounged a rather large inheritance bouncing checks on luxury cars and a film company he ran or pretended to run and had then kicked his great aunt out of her massive apartment on the Champs-Élysées to pay his debts and get himself out of prison a few months after JC was born. Delphine who came from a much less privileged background had her own story it turns out and had been a kept women for years with an allowance for clothes and housing from a married man.

"I don't want him to turn into me," Pierre says in explanation when JC heads off to use the toilet but this too conveniently favours their own finances.

Pierre pulls out a pipe and stuffs it with a rather nice smelling tobacco and Delphine pulls out a delicate cigarette from a beautiful case she attaches to a lorgnette. Maebh leans back to savour her meal and the golden apricot hues glistening in the mirrors. Two couples at a nearby table are arguing about privatization and center-right politics with loud conviction. The man with hair swept loosely back over crown and a slightly feminine voice draws her attention most because he's so handsome.

"The Socialists have become elitist snobs but Jacques Chirac—*Le Presi•ent—Non, jamais!* He would undo everything France has spent decades achieving," he says.

Maebh is happy her French is improving enough that she can catch some of their conversation. She takes her last sip of whatever simple but rare champagne it is they ordered feeling so removed from reality in a charmed way she almost doesn't notice she's being given the most careful instructions.

"You will need to control the finances," Delphine says, "and never let him touch your wallet or bank account." Maebh blushes and wonders how she knows.

"I don't think I can help it," she says. "I hope he will learn some restraint and I don't want to spend my life adding up my husband's numbers."

"Then the marriage is ruined," Delphine says.

Maebh is upset Delphine wants her to babysit and hasn't saved her instructions for her son.

"He was always unreasonable and never did what he was told," she says. "As a child he woke us constantly with his nightmares and how were we to get to work in the morning with all that crying? We tried to teach him consequences and when he wouldn't prepare for his baccalauréat, we refused to take him to the dentist but nothing worked."

Maebh gasps. They have tried so hard to convince her that JC's failures are his and his alone when this is precisely what she had supposed. Now wondering why they spend so much energy absolving themselves of any connection to this, she is beginning to think their selfish indifference had some part in it.

"Oh how he made me suffer," says Delphine pulling gently on her cigarette. Pierre nods in agreement and takes Delphine's hand. They hide behind well-bred decency and belittle their child to mask their discomfort.

Pierre, perhaps more aware, talks about being allowed to indulge fantasies as a young man himself, which he could never have fulfilled, and how he wanted to caution JC.

They want to take Maebh under their wing, woo her to their cause but her stomach is a bit upset from the strong coffee and the wine has now made her sad. She looks at JC when he comes back to catch the tail end of the conversation with pity. They care only for the disappointment he brought them and she sees JC's pretensions crinkle up inside and her heart wells up.

Pierre helps Maebh into her tweed jacket which she's too flushed to need and they walk out gaily in the late afternoon just behind the handsome man and his wife from the other table. Both groups kiss and shake hands in the French way and head off as if there were nothing other to do on a Sunday but loll for hours over debate and food. It's the French way—full blown discord but if the meal is good you go home friends.

The miracle of sharing a table of well-lit ambiance in JC's family cures bad blood, even if temporarily, Maebh muses, as well as it has in hers and they will lunch once a month from then on with his parents at their apartment in the 15th. Delphine cooks even better than many of the restaurants and they watch the films of Godard, Renoir and Truffaut till late in the evening.

"I hate Goddard," Maebh says, "The men are all victims and the women vilified as the cause of their problems but Renoir and Truffaut are very '*sympa*' ."

"You've only seen a few films and off you go with criticism," Delphine says.

They clean up together brushing the crumbs off the antique table and the linen tablecloth with a tiny silver brush and shovel. Their apartment is small but has thick Persian rugs, not the worn out kind Maebh's parents have, and other inherited furnishings that hint at the more gentile life that should have been theirs.

"Inherited," Pierre says that word with a mark of pride as he dries the dishes, aproned with tea towel in hand.

"You look adorable," Maebh says.

"Snobbery and all," adds JC.

"My father has never washed a dish in his life."

Pierre tucks the tea towel into his apron and carefully arranges the scalloped wine glasses into neat rows in the antique cabinet, unsure of whether this is a compliment. He always drives them home and each time as they make the turn round Arc de Triomph—Frenchy little cars jagging deftly in and out of nonexistent lanes—Maebh feels fairly satisfied with life.

—

Their wedding happens a bit last minute in the southwest near Toulouse at the country house JC's parents hope to retire to in a few years. Maebh's parents fly over from Dublin to cook pheasant and venison they buy in Albi and her mum makes a three-tier cake with terracotta roses. Chris and Elsa, Maebh's friends from university studying at the Sorbonne for a year come too and stay in the annex house next door that JC's parents bought because they didn't want any neighbours peering their noses into their garden. Maebh invited Dubi but never heard back from him. Djamila is there and her new boyfriend. Roisin and James stay in Dublin though and Sinead is working in Toronto. It's just a whoever is in town type of affair.

It's cold and sprinkled with crinkly snow over the rolling hills and sloped roofs of Gaillac. The snow seems out of place to Maebh but not as much as all the money thrown around in their honour. She has refused to grasp fully that she is celebrating a marriage perhaps because hers is not one to celebrate. She wears a tacky veil Elsa picked up at Tati and a long vintage red velvet dress she found for a mere 150 francs at the Pus market that fit her to perfection. Her father asks if she wants a string quartet instead of whether she was sure she wanted a ceremony but does turn to JC man to man. One moment they are discussing the opening line of *The Outsider*:

"Aujourd'hui, maman est morte," her father says. "It's so important that it's *maman* and not *ma mere*. You know! You know!"

And then his eyes stick out and he slams the table."So how, JC, are you going to, you know, as a man provide for this marriage," he asks.

JC stares at his glass.

"That's what men do," her father continues.

"A man is more than a wallet," JC says.

"Oh Cal, let them be!" says Maebh's mum.

But Maebh's dad has taken JC to the bar and seen first hand how in defiance of 'drink like a man' culture he bounces off the walls and bums drink after drink. Maebh who holds perhaps too much in distorted awe, both the JC drunk and her father's you-drive-home-without-even-fumbling-with-the-car-keys-to-pay-the-mortgage type of drunk, is still annoyed that he thinks money conversations exclusive to men when she's the one making it. She's irritated further because in the middle of a drunken discussion on American political interference her dad had just the day before hinted that she no longer need pursue plans for graduate school or poetry now she had found a husband.

"They'll find someone else to blame the need for a nuclear arsenal on," her father had said.

"A cold war is always better than Vietnam," JC had replied.

"Not if you were living in Pinochet's Chile!"

"El pueblo unido jamás será vencido," JC had said pacing around the room.

"Thatcher and Reagan," her father spits.

"Come and see the blood in the streets."

"Neruda was posted in Madrid during the Spanish Civil War."

"My rosa pequeña—mais eeeeeeve—petite poetess," JC had said with hands outstretched in front of his face.

"Maebh has no need for poetry now that she's getting married, or for university either," her father had said.

The anti-war 'humanist' politics of both her father and husband made old fashioned assumptions about her life hard to comprehend. In fact, her father's sometime revelations about women and art shock Maebh so much she has buried her heartbreak many miles beneath a rational comeback. His was a love is all a woman needs, man-only humanism. So to mask her many confusions and feelings and how she might have wished her father would grab her by the arm and take her away from this marriage, Maebh says what must shut the whole conversation about JC's fitness as a husband down.

"We aren't sure this marriage is going to work but we will go for it anyway just like you did," Maebh had said.

"So, it's meant to be," her father had shrugged as the snow melts from the trees with persistent drip. "But it will end in disaster."

So he does care, Maebh had thought.

Her parents were married at eighteen and twenty-two because they were expecting Maebh. Except there's was a marriage of genuine love and lust on both sides and her father had had a good job—not that they hadn't been through their share of bitterness and strife.

"Love is a blind thing," Maebh thinks sipping her breakfast tea—"generation after abandoned generation, you half hug and eat meals together ignoring pains you have no idea how to stop." Maebh doesn't know why she can't just stop this marriage herself without expecting her father to do it for her. The snow feels more than her heart which seems on auto-pilot to a crash landing of its own volition.

The wedding is nearly cancelled, however. They had not applied for the permit properly but the justice of the peace takes a shine to them:

"Don't you worry," he says. "I will get your beautiful children married."

Maebh giggles through the "I do's" by JC's side while her father struggles with the camera—his hands shaking. Maebh will see the giggles, shaking hands and the lack of a marriage permit as a sign of what should never have been and will promise to never throw away future get-out-of-jail-free cards again. She does think about how abandoning him at the altar would have put a sour mood on the party, and of all the wasted cooking and cleaning.

She already has a massive vodka hangover that won't go away before they even sit down to dinner. JC gives a speech about his fleshy Mais-Eve and mum who didn't even get a second to put any makeup on rushes about serving. Maebh stares down the cobbled path out the window where the moon hangs full and low stone white over the hamlet. It does feel as if she is, in fact, stepping into rightfully mapped out steps—steps she wished weren't for her.

The next day, she opens all kinds of envelopes filled with unexpected checks from relatives that will get wasted on food and rent. She wonders how what seems so right could be so wrong. There have been other ways out, other paths crossed, lives she could have lived. She could see them before her like a jigsaw. There had been encounters those first few months with other men out in Paris even on the plane over from Prague and glimpses into a different life. A filmmaker from Hong Kong had admired her dainty feet and bought her meals before she got her first pay-check and a photographer from Chile had showed her his portfolio and asked to take her photos for a show—"no, no nudes," he had assured but Maebh had refused more because she hadn't found his photos that good. An art dealer near Pompidou had told her she has the saddest face he had ever seen. She had even been invited by a well-dressed Middle Eastern man to model the luxury clothes he proposed to buy her.

Elsa comes by, "You look like Michelle Pfeiffer in *Dangerous Liasons* but I can tell you aren't okay?"

"Yeah!"

"You should have eloped," she says. "Way more your style."

"I'm so glad you and Chris came," Maebh says knowing that eloping wouldn't have changed much. She and Elsa have been friends only a year or two and are not even very close but they were her only friends from Toronto at the event. They had hung out quite a bit at university in Hart House Cafe. Maebh has never had any long term close friends—maybe she expects too much from friendship. Maybe you need to know who you are first.

"Here's a bunch of dresses that will never fit me again and you'll be skinny forever," Elsa says handing her a pretty package decorated with Titian's *Reclining Venus* wrapping paper and a huge gold bow. "I have nothing else to give you."

"Ah sweet!" Maebh says. "Are you and Chris going to get married?"

"Well, actually yeah so I can get an Irish passport like Chris and stay here forever," she laughs.

"Chris is Irish?" Maebh asks.

"His grandfather is," Elsa says.

"Oh! I'd love it if you could both stay here."

"We will have to go home to get married but hope to come back after."

Maebh had gotten Elsa a job at Languainc which she had had to turn down because she couldn't get a work visa.

"That really sucks about the papers thing."

"Yeah you are lucky you get to stay and you didn't even need to get married for that, you silly fool. Are you going to take his name?"

"Maybe!"

"Maebh Danjou—how rich," says Elsa. "But I'm not giving up Elsa Okun for Mrs. White."

"What is it about the place that draws us here?"

"It's ages old resistant and scintillating," says Elsa.

"Scintillating," Maebh laughs and squeezes Elsa's hand.

She wants to go to bed but her father and JC have started on the bushmills so she slips out the back door and walks up through the hamlet to the old water fountain. She does find a kind of ease there and the fresh air revives her as she sits at the stone wall in her black velvet hat and the cape Djamila lent her. Women would have come here to wear down their hands washing clothes and maybe escape the house so she goes through a list of vain things about her life that make her smile and what it might be like to marry any of the other men who have shown her attention in Paris.

She has a job and a husband and Paris at twenty-four. People seem impressed with her here and she never had so much attention in Toronto. Her new boss gives her the most elegant clients and the woman in the local restaurant where they go with the vouchers she gets from work stares and stares every time. This attention will stop soon enough, partly because she will be less the doe-eyed newcomer but more probably because she will start to look as terrible as she feels.

There is nowhere to go in this hamlet—no trails, shops or fields to wander through before you hit the small cliff behind and the main road below. It is almost claustrophobic Maebh thinks walking back down to the party. Her silvery silhouette stretches out just ahead in the moonlight like a woman from another era. A woman who had not the choices she in fact has.

Her mum is in the kitchen washing dishes and Maebh feels guilty but Djamila puts a flower wreath in her hair as soon as she opens the garden gate and Delphine is holding the sugar rose cake.

"There she is," says Djamila.

"The roses match the red of your dress perfectly," Delphine says.

"You have the perfect blushing bride, JC," Djamila adds beaming.

"Everyone is so happy for us," JC says kissing her and clapping his hands.

Her father has the camera again and comes in for the perfect shots—the red dress, white sprinkle snow and medieval buildings don't hurt—JC in white shirt with black tie and tweed cap. These will be the most beautiful photos of her since the photos her father took of her as a child. Marriage brings photos. There will be a whole slew of ugly ones the next few years but the beautiful ones from the wedding which did not thank goodness in any way reveal her anxieties will fade them out. Maybe she is more hopeful than she realizes. JC will rip these photos almost in two one day after an argument but Maebh will glue them up and hope all the same.

7

The apartment sweeps round a corner at a soft angle on Rue Carpeaux. It has three large French windows that follow the course of the sun. It's a Paris sun – damp filtered with golden pink undertones. *Le Cimitiere de Montmartre* is just below and the apartments around belong to a woman who disappeared sometime ago and another who is deaf. The guy upstairs sells weed. Birds sweep from tree to tree - the only sound you hear on the balconies, in a Paris that seems reserved only for them.

Being married even to the wrong man implies the kind of perfection in itself she knew it would. She's pregnant too already but it's saying that word "my husband" – not the man himself or the real ring his parents eventually buy for her that seals the sentiment. She stands fingering it on her middle finger. It's too big and will never be adjusted which helps makes the marriage less of a thing.

Velvet Underground*'s Sunday Morning* is playing even though it's Monday and JC is still sleeping. There's an ashtray by his side of the bed littered with stray unfinished cigarettes she bends down to attend to. She'll need a cloth even to clean up. She admires his alcoholic snore and anosmia. There is also his matchstick leg scattered with dark hairs peeking from the cover and how resentful she is the pregnancy has not convinced him to smoke on the balcony.

"I'm pregnant!" she says. It has happened again this beautiful state no one need remain in and she expects him to insist on a termination. She's ready herself to sign it away - "dear lovely child – I'm blushing with love at the thought of you but we two delinquents just aren't ready."

"Great!" he says blushing too but with an even deeper satisfaction than hers. They are married and her job teaching executives with a private language school is respectable and pays enough. They also get health care and government help with their rent. It's just a bit soon. The sparse pieces of furniture they have come from the street. The room is barren like an avant garde film set – beige, grey and white. The walls smudged and cuffed.

"Should we keep it?"

"Why not?"

"But..." and he looks at her – blithe - there are no buts. Except, rinsing the cigarette ash from the cloth and soaking it in burning dish soap water to remove the smell, there always is a residue. The smoke curls round your evening and is wretched by next morning. But Maebh would accompany his blithe and wants to cure herself of tending to residues so another faulty decision is made.

They had been to see Buster Keaton's *The General* last night with Chris and Elsa. Elsa and Maebh both had hair pulled high in a bun but Elsa is bosomed Modigliani to her flowing Titian. At least that is what they discover, when they purchase the postcards after the show at Palais Royale and they paste them at their respective bathroom mirrors to frame mutual admiration and a certain reassurance that their respective physical differences minimize any stealing of each other's man.

After the film, they go out for drinks at *Sancerre* and then spend the rest of the evening chasing fire fighters up and round the steps at *Sacre Coeur*. Maebh misses out on the fun because she has to get up for work and the general fatigues of pregnancy. This is a good thing because she's drinking much less than she was in Prague but still a glass from time to time more than zero, which was her usual.

She places the clean ashtray hum humming Niko's *femme fatale*. Irritated but at peace with irritations. The hormones have her resigned but happy. JC spends his days painting without bringing money in but life is taking her somewhere which is better than nowhere. They feel a glow on them at gallery openings and dinners and sidewalks still fade when he has her round his arm. His friends lavish her with compliments and the tall good looking one with a girlfriend moves in to pass her his business card,

"*Tu es fausse maigre*", he whispers in her ear which seems to mean fake skinny.

They are far from the smoked salmon life they enjoyed in Prague but Paris is not such a bad city to be poor in. If they are poor or spoilt brats not as able to indulge as they'd like to. JC's habit of insulting people and a desperateness they eventually give off has invitations dwindle though the long nights trailing the Canal St. Martin to Stalingrad and Pigalle still charm.

Maebh looks at JC as he stirs on the mattress set up on the raised part of the floor in one corner of the apartment. She stares again at his leg – thinner and more hairless than hers. It stretches out now entirely from the paisley quilt her mother brought over along with the teapot and four blue flowered dishes she had got on the Summerhill strip in Toronto. Those same legs appear, cartoonish, in his paintings with naked light bulbs hanging from the ceiling. She now recognizes the copied elements in his work from Philip Guston, Jasper Johns and Willem de Kooning. They have cartoonish light fixtures hanging from sconces on the walls in their apartment and she doesn't understand why he wouldn't copy those instead. She finds his obsession with American kitsch intriguing and the French obsession with McDonalds popping up everywhere even more so. He persists with his Adam and Eve project. The pork chop is his new *objet* and he puts it on paintings of his bare chests to look vaguely like a female with a camouflage background. He calls this porkchop Adam's rib and porkchop is also his new word for her. Maebh is excited about what might come of his efforts but he seems pinched and to have lost something he had when he was jumping the fence at the Ecole Superior de Beaux Arts to set up a studio for himself in an abandoned shed. What a cheek he had parking himself so far away from his professors and fellow students. But she admires that about him and worries more about stifling his spark than her own.

A friend from New York had come by last week with a large work JC had left there that another friend wanted to buy. She had recognized it from one of the postcards he showed her in Prague.

"This is Anika", white white Swedish blonde like one half of ABBA and ever stylish. "The woman who bought my *Telemaque*.

You know the large self-portrait of me trying to suck my own penis".

She had nodded remembering it well. It was a very good painting and as far as she could tell his best. JC long and naked on a dark blue oval background – delight on his face, penis smacked on there.

"Telemaque is trying to find his father – you know Ulysses which is as impossible as auto fellatio."

Anika had rolled out this other painting on the floor. "It's like a Jean-Michel Basquiat", she says pointing out the comic book collage and graffiti aspects.

"C'est de la merde" JC had said and proceeded, ignoring the pleas to "stop" from both Anika and Maebh, to cut it smaller and smaller. And then there was nothing of interest left. "Your friend can have it for 500F", JC had said standing in a shell of himself. Anika had taken it mostly because she felt she had to and would have paid triple for the original.

Maebh sorts through her clothes for the day and notices JC stirring on the mattress.

"He's loosing it," she thinks.

He looks up at Maebh all of sudden awake, "mais Eve, don't leave *ma grosse* pork chop," he says.

"Stop calling me that!" Although as other men found her too thin, it rather makes her feel desirable - "Look at me, I'm Betty Blue!" she says tip toeing by with slight show off prance. She sits beside him on the raised bit of flooring to put on her tights and shoes. She notices with some annoyance the long hairs on her own legs - lighter but denser than JC's - so she rushes over to the bathroom to shave them.

"Why do I care so much about appearances," she says over the on and off of the hand shower . "It takes time to become what you feel for each other, to become more than what you look like."

"What are you muttering about?" asks JC.

"That the act of undressing is most beautiful when it's an expression of wanting to be as close to someone as possible - that you undress to reveal your true self and you trace the lines of each others' bodies to feel their soul beneath you."

He's not listening so it's easy to continue. He closes his eyes again with one arm raised back and drums his fingers on the wall by his head. She is as invisible to him as she has always been but that brings certain advantages. Her words disperse into emptiness she's learning to formulate without judgement. On the raised bit of flooring for the bed, she sits again and puts a bit of cream on her legs looking at JC's silly porkchop painting hanging above and wondering where his confidence comes from.

"The Bible has two creation myths. In one, Adam and Eve build a life together and in the second Adam does so alone until finally he feels worthy of a partner to share things with."

JC opens his eyes and starts laughing. "Look at you with your Bible! Are you joining the cloister now my little nun?"

"I might!" She pulls up her tights – not too sheer, not too thick.

"*Ca te va bien*!" he says admiring. "Maybe you could come over and sit on me instead."

"Or you could dress and get a job," she says with a laugh or is it frustration - not very loud so she thinks he doesn't hear but still she has never actually come out and said this before.

She continues on with her talk exploring aloud ideas and missing university conversation too and the chance to ramble on about things that no one ever talks about.

"The feminists challenge the first version of the myth because it makes women a secondary character in history but what if Adam is not man but the self in search of self-realization and Eve not woman but the genderless partner we seek to woo. The second myth is interesting because it suggests that we are all Adam's forging some kind of an identity on our own first before we are worthy of our "Eve" or "life partner".

JC is up and about now making his coffee in the kitchen. He's prancing about still drunk from last night in only a t-shirt flailing about, what he likes to call, his third leg. It looks rather substantial on his thin frame.

"Where is the lighter?" he says.

"In the ashtray," she says fumbling over to where it sits neatly in it beside the trousers he's thrown by the bed. She brings it over to him to shut him and the cupboard banging up.

"And that's why eating from the tree of knowledge and the nudity in the myth is important as a symbol of seeing the cruel reality of experience and why this comes with suffering and a desire to cover up and the love that comes of a desire to know the other and trust is what takes the edge off the anxiety."

She sighs, losing her train of thought and feels the words twist up tighter and tighter away from how lucid her understanding of them appears in her mind but keeps trying to rework them to rework history essentially in a way that excludes women less and helps take away how little they seem to have accomplished. She's already but not completely aware yet of the role maternity might have played in women's absence from history but maternity is not something she expects to deter her from anything. She also doesn't realize that her interpretation of these words holds a kind of wisdom she has not been able to follow herself.

She puts on her coat and some lipstick. "You look so much better now," JC says and she curtsies deciding to take it as a compliment because it's true.

And then just as she moves in to kiss him good-bye and as JC prepares to jump back into bed with toast and book, the fact that he has time to lounge about and devote to his profession because she's out working to pay the bills hits harder and she says what she'd merely whispered before, louder and more pitchy than she expects.

"Why don't you get a job?"

He puts his coffee by the bed and ignores her so she elaborates gently and then not so gently about how much better off they'd be, how they could both work part-time and still pursue art and how unfair it is.

"Love isn't about money," he says.

"But someone has to make it."

"That's your choice," he says.

"But I share it and you expect me to."

"Because you love me."

"But I'm tired."

"Oh shut up!"

"And you're just lying there."

And by now her voice has turned strident and then he turns around and does what he knows will silence her. He slaps her. Her head whips hard and wells with immediate tears and it hurts. She half sees him, not much heavier than her, and that she could hit him back but the callous in him stops her like the time he ripped up her brand new copy of *Crime and Punishment* - the one she'd never finish - because she was upset he kept reading it while she was throwing up that morning in the bathroom. Worse, she expects him to look shocked or apologize like it was an act of passion he regrets that just happened of itself but he looks pleased as if the slap was carefully planned and well deserved and he doesn't even consider coming over to where she's hiding away in the bathroom. She dries her face with a towel and covers the redness with some powder and then she opens the door to leave.

She walks down the four flights of stairs – hollow sounds - round by the cemetery up to Rue Lepic. The bare brick walls go on and on. She heads up rue Gaulaincourt wishing she could stop at some café for a read rather than continue on to the language school.

She measures her steps up the hill – and a one two three four - fired up, smushed down. He expects her to pay her way and his. And that's what she fears she can't escape or even just yet assess so she makes excuses. Housewife - ugh - she remembers the term in cursive by her mother's ridiculously childlike passport picture. But she's pregnant and in a kind of joy from that and then there's the joy of Paris and its everyday routine which lulls. She lets the lulling work its way over her senses.

It's February but there's no need for heavy scarves and boots. The weather, like every shop in the 18th arrondissement, is civilized. Bunches of wild flowers sit at a stall. There are thin grey chickens with heads bobbing and feet strung up in the front windows. Then there's the shop with caramelized fruit tarts. When you buy apples the vendor might ask if you prefer them sweet or sour, soft or crunchy and when you plan to eat them before he chooses them for you.

"I'll give you this for free," the vendor with the North African accent says winking at her and this makes her feel taken care of for a few seconds. "It's delicious but the skin is a bit wrinkly so no one will buy it". He wraps the fruit up in a small paper bags and twists the ends in curls. She takes the ugly one in her hand and bites into it – he's right or maybe she's just grateful.

Her fingers round the apple aren't freezing as they would have been in Toronto and the stress saved from battling the elements here might account for the extra energy the French have to ensure life is something to be enjoyed. Climate, geography and culture seem to live in a kind of harmony here, she thinks. The gulf-stream which runs by Britain, Amsterdam and France could be a greater gift to civilization than imagined and the calm eroded landscapes that cater less to natural disaster too. She feels safe here or free in her mind to ponder on more than how she might stop from slipping on an icy sidewalk, especially now that she knows where her next meal is coming from.

And so the ebb and flow of Paris takes over, she forgets what makes no sense in her life and a bliss fills her steps as she walks where and how she pleases - maybe this street or that to work. Age old Paris is the movie scene of life she becomes part of - invisible and one with time. There is the unknown to stumble on everyday and no one knows her here to look at her with a recognition that might remind her of herself. She walks down Abbesses past the Moulin Rouge, the naked lady clubs and through the ninth *arrondissement* to *Trinite* where she teaches. It's downhill all the way after Montmartre, her arms freely at her sides and her shoes light on the pavement – flowers, decay, epicurism, bare breasts.

The day passes easily from this. The lessons are planned for her and her students lovely to converse with. They work for companies that make under highway tunnels for wildlife to cross and all kinds of other professions she never knew existed. She even gets a paid for prix-fix lunch which is her only proper meal that first month before she gets a paycheck.

She's with her student of Sicilian origin that afternoon. Paris might be as multicultural as Toronto but no one goes on about it.

She was told he lost his wife and child to a car accident while on holiday and to be especially sweet. She notices the loss all over his face even though he never stops smiling. Today, they work on the conditional and the lesson has a picture of The Acropolis, a beach in Bali, San Francisco and a cruise ship in Alaska.

"Where would you go, if you won a free holiday?" she says.

"Greece," he says.

"Me too!" she smiles. "If…" and she motions that he should finish the sentence and then reminds him that in the more dreamy 2nd conditional, the verb in the secondary clause takes the past tense.

"Those are Doric columns," he says. "Do you know the other types?"

"Ionic and Corinthian", she says going back to renaissance art class with Professor Sohm. She read the textbook from cover to cover and Vasari and had taken a year off school the year before with London as a base from which to see the works in the flesh but she still only got a B-. Writing Masaccio 1420 or so wasn't her forte. But she had recognized the dynamic Renaissance brushstroke, the figures increasingly infused with movement and the evolution of Catholicism and atheism mythologized in the less god-fearing artist.

Her student finishes his conditional sentences and then turns the grammar hand-out over and draws three points in a line. "These are the peaks of western culture – the Greeks, the Renaissance and Modernism."

"I've heard that before," she says, "but never outlined quite so exactly."

"I'm an engineer," he says. "Most of what we have today starts with Galileo - with science."

"Maebh nods in agreement delighted to be having this conversation with an executive designer for a machine part she has never heard of and that they both know a Giotto from a Raphael and a Cezanne from a Picasso.

"Don't you think the peaks are a bit high," she says.

He laughs and says probably but that we shouldn't underestimate the progress in science and art that happened during these times.

"Galileo was much smarter than poor Bruno who was burned at the stake," he says.

"Surely they knew the earth was round much earlier."

"True, but keeping this locked up inside you with a wink at the heavens was not easy," he says.

By the time their class is over, Maebh has forgotten the morning slap entirely and her student also might have stepped away some from his troubles.

But then, she sees Rupert the computer guy.

"What's your lay-about husband up to today?" he says. "You could have had me, you know."

"Oh, but you deserve someone as posh and small-minded as yourself," she says but with affection knowing that it is her loss in some ways but maybe not all.

He looks after her concerned and that feels syrupy. "I'd make my pregnant wife breakfast in bed and let her lie in it all day," he says after her.

That does sound nice but then you are trapped in a dollhouse existence.

"I told everyone in the office to keep their hands off - that you were mine to conquer," he adds finally with a touch of hurt resentment.

"Come find me - big and fat - on my tower of ivory," she waves cupping her would be baby belly with her other hand.

Poor Rupert will fight the company to get her severance pay when it goes bust a year from now. JC for all his vulgarity would never talk so but then enough women fell at his feet when he looked at them, he didn't have to resort to such strategies to woo them.

She runs down the stairs - red thick carpet, luxurious underfoot and then the surge of Paris on her face. Pregnancy has brought an unexpected vitality into her life - her skin is milky and at three months so, her body seems to have come into itself. However, it's the sense of purpose she feels which most surprises and that worries that have plagued since puberty have dissipated. A child is forming within her and like a tree shaking chestnut boughs, her mind has bowed before the nature it can only allow triumph. Her body craves the child but she's not sure she does - a whole slew of unknown fears about maternity rises before her and this is a battle that has been going on within her since she got her first period during the grade 8 beach party. Even, inclined as she might be, to revolt in slight disgust by the lulling moon of maternity, she is fuelled by the drug of it into a contentment she wishes she could bottle spray on to assuage all angst.

She stops off on her way home to get a proper bra fitted at a shop on Chausee D'Antin. Her mum was frantic when she said she didn't have one. She pulls out a black lacy thing from one of the bins on sale outside which looks well enough like something that might fit but the sales lady insists on measuring her. When she tells her she's pregnant, the sales lady clucks disapprovingly at the delicate lace object she chose and brings her a white cotton apparatus. Maebh ignores her sensibility and watches how stately well-dressed she is over what is surely something more risque underneath. She appreciates the time she takes with her but the black lace shows off her throat so much better and is cheaper. Maebh gets her to come into the change room to cut off the tags while she's wearing it because she's blushing and can't bear to take it off and notices as she walks out the store with the cherished thing cradling her upper regions that she and the sales lady have amused each other.

She wanders about, not too lost as there's a metro stop every few streets to guide her. They have a large vintage city map tacked to the toilet wall she studies intently hoping for an imprint of the streets that wind about in an arbitrary way. "You find your way by moving from monument to monument," JC says. And Maebh is surprised to find Paris more contained than she would have expected and that she can cover large chunks of it easily in an evening.

JC is painting at his studio in an abandoned house in the thirteenth and is never home till very late. A Vietnamese gang has been threatening him though and, either because they buy the place or have the resources to better pretend to, they'll throw him and his stuff out and then he'll paint not without massive temper tantrums in the left corner at the apartment.

In any case, there's some sun today which is unusual so she's in no hurry to get home. She finds herself in a nondescript street that the sunset sets off with cinematic rencontre. Some men on ladders fix street lamps to one side and it seems she has stepped into the frames of a set. She sees a copy of Baudelaire's *La Spleen de Paris* staring out at her inside a windowsill. It too seems part of the staging. She rubs her stomach wishing she could take the book to turn the pages and let the words swell out as they may like pictures. She finds herself this evening moving not by brain, heart or sexual desire but some other organ. A flânneuse like her, what need has she for words she cannot remember precisely except how readily they were absorbed. Empty handed - possibilities are open more to what footsteps overtake in the mind.

There is one particular poem in *Les Fleur du Mal,* she thinks, about the imagined experience one can create in an instant crossing glances with a passerby – that can make of life, like the map of Paris, an arbitrary array of paths and happenstance. In those seconds another life flashes by. The man entering stage left, for example, seems imbued with a similar aesthetic. As he comes closer, Maebh notices that it is Rupert Everett, the British actor, out about in lure like her – adrift with sales.

"Words, words," she says, "let them fly, let me catch them."

The dark shade stains on the buildings, the smell of urine among the plantain trees. She and Rupert look gauzy but intent at each other, surprised at what they recognize. She knows she doesn't have the right body parts but beyond that a genderless attraction flowing before physical touch wakes you, pulls her down to its lair. This is Paris for her. A beauty anyone might kidnap for themselves. And then Rupert is gone.

She hits the steep slopes into the 18th arrondissement and makes it to the top panting a bit. She picks up some pink roses that smell of absolutely nothing but last for weeks but instead of heading downhill towards the cemetery and the abandoned hospital which is now an artists co-op she turns right swinging the bouquet with each step and stops off at – La Sancerre - her favorite café with the handsome waiter who looks a bit like the TV puppet Alf.

There's a seat by the window and people passing by and Maebh puts the bag of verveine into the pot of water and her fork through the tartelette au pomme avec boule de glace. The Georges Brassens song playing - *Les Passants* - speaks like the very same Baudelaire poem she had just been thinking about. There's a whole lifetime here and there in a man's glance through a window or on the street, a flicker of time is all time. So she pulls out a notebook feeling as if most perfectly at ease in her destiny, to take down her Rupert Everett experience. The little pale words in her notebook set off the apple slices rippled rectangle through the tartlette and the ice cream smoothed over it mirrored in the glass of the cafe. Loving these moments compensates for not feeling loved or loving entirely herself. You can love life without loving yourself.

Then she gets side tracked by to do lists. Bra - check, enquire at the Sorbonne re: a masters degree – one day soon. She also tries to write a letter to Dubi, she never sends and then she'll be hurt he stops writing back. He got a film job and is working with her sister Sinead. She wonders if he ever wrote his play but everyone in Toronto is working in film. She scribbles a bunch of numbers. Salary 10,000F a month (maybe), rent 3500F, telephone and all that stuff "?" Food and other stuff "??" They have enough and save by cooking at home mostly and buying very little till the card is declined and they eat less till she gets an advance.

A man leans over. "Are you writing a poem?"

"No, I'm trying to make a budget," she laughs pleased he guessed she might have been.

They get into a short conversation about what she's doing here. He's from Lebanon and delivers cement trucks for a living.

"I am looking for an English tutor," he says. This happens a few times, sometimes she calls but it always means a hoped for affair. She's even been offered financial help which does seem tempting especially when the man is sweet and attractive.

She heads off home following the descent of rue Gaulaincourt and the faint sun lines. There should be enough money to pay the rent and feed them so she puts finances out of her head and she will find a way to write things down when she figures out what the things are.

They say it is impossible to be an artist and not poor these days but TS Eliot had his bank job. In the meantime, there's the Proust – she can feel it in her bag. She's reading the second *tome* in French with limited comprehension but much triumph now that her bad French is no longer answered with bad English.

At her apartment, she walks up the four flights of stairs. JC is nowhere in sight. She hardly ever sees him that first year and he's not the type to apologize so today she's relieved. She puts the tiny pink roses in a vase on the wooden fold-up table they found on the street along with the small two-seater couch she has no idea how they lugged up themselves. She puts her coat on the rather nice wooden armchair a woman on the first floor gave her when she visited for tea a few times. She had even spent the night in her spare bed once when JC fell so soundly asleep he didn't hear her knocking home late from the café she worked in over the summer. The lady doesn't talk to her anymore and had lashed out at how she hadn't visited enough but Maebh keeps the chair.

There's a mirror in one corner and she sits in front of it contemplating her fuller figure. Ballerina lines were lovely but the small bumps on her chest weren't much.

"Breasts are only good because when you push them up they look like bums," JC says. "You go bing bing with them for five seconds and then you are done."

In the mirror, there's something in how Maebh positions herself that changes everything or it's the desire her body feels to look at itself. She is kneeling down at a forty-five degree angle watching the late afternoon colour in her face. She holds herself like a pin-up and notices the line of black lace under her scoop neck dress so she shakes her shoulders a bit and hunches them, watching how the dress falls off to reveal a bit more bra. She keeps repeating this and pulls the bra down a bit more each time and then lets the straps fall off her shoulders. Her body, her breasts becomes more than themselves - the areola pinker and larger than normal. Red dress, black lace, pink nipple. She puts her fingers down her underwear, drawn to touch herself in a way she never has before. Men have kissed her there determined something will happen to no avail. She's touched herself too without experiencing anything either. But this time it is different. A shift into some kind of adulthood - a vague sense of independence and satisfaction - all the compliments from strange men - has made her feel beautiful and heralded her introduction to onanism.

She stretches out - the room flushed - not sure why she had never been able to do this before. The urge had been there but riled up too strong to unravel. At least she had orgasmed for a time with Maxim but then never with any other man and not with JC either.

The white sheet curtains just washed flap whiter than ever against the dirty walls and JC's Adam with porkchop painting holds its place beside them. The uncooked cartoon porkchop which is supposed to be Eve looks almost as if it could be a female body but the whole beyond the central idea lacks finesse and expression. The phone rings but she ignores it. JC never calls. Maybe Eve had a better time with the apple in her mouth and the snake in her ear and we are all walking about with uncooked pork chops at out chests. Maebh feels the slap again on her cheek - just barely. It should matter - it should shock and terrify her enough to get her out of her marriage. JP feels it was an accepted and deserved act. Maebh saw that on his face and this hurts more even than the slap but she doesn't move. She's sidetracked by too many other questions. Who she is and why she accepts what she accepts. Who she is and is that the same as what she is or every sensation she can and must feel. Pleasure, pain and frustration fester at the heart of existence.

Maebh drifts off in a sleepy state. Her dress as she lies there debauched takes on a glossy sheen and the afternoon sun washes the walls hard yellow. She pulls one leg up as if to take a photograph like the Guy Bourdin women in Vogue magazine – bodies twisted lacquered. The curtains keep flickering in the window frame draft, the long glass panes rattle in flecks of soot on the baseboard edges. She feels cut up but very attune. She is finding herself in every feeling existence can conjure up for her. Whatever random steps she has taken through whatever random streets, she feels sure it was to find this pose - half folded up in paisley quilt, waiting for a signal, waiting to be woken.

She hides in her corner with blank purpose, pregnant but unaware of the challenges ahead or the rightful needs of her child and how this will change her life. The child will be a child like her in her lonely corners. The child was conceived and will be fed in this corner Maebh now just masturbated in for the first time - as if she is mother before she is woman: all things rolling as they do in inexplicable order.

8

The face on the book is han• some
seen upsi• e • own from the foot of the be•
Daddy reads aloud.

Beckett comes from Northern Irelan• like them
but Beckett lives in France now. They in East York.
"No one buys you a drink here."

When the play ends
She asks the right question
and daddy throws her in the air.
She hovers like an angel in her nighty.

"That's it!" he says.
"What are they waiting for?"

When she turns four, she is rea• ing Lewis Carroll
She • oes not know if she is too young or too ol•.
Daddy stops holding her
it isn't appropriate.

They move to a house with a veranda
where the purple perfume tree is in bloom.
Sweet baby leaves.
"They are bu• s!"

A single word can drown a thing in precision.

In the afternoon, mummy lies in bed.
She sells cigarettes
her bunny costume slung over the chair.
Maebh puts the ears on and the little tail.

Her manager
says mummy's lips aren't full enough
but yours are Maebh.

She tells mummy that at school they say her legs are pink
and mummy strokes them.
Something she never knew existed.
She wishes she would again.

She sifts through the basket of cigarettes
black and gold crinkly packaging fills the silence
and the Playboy magazines under the desk
It felt nice in her underwear when she looked at them.

She wanders
until daddy comes home.
He tickles her feet, throws the big leather jacket over her
but heads up to mum.
Daddy's jacket is heavy
And she crawls with it over to her corner.

The charcoal sketch on the wall by the chimney speaks.
"You're here again."

She shivers.
"Alone."

Lines of cement circle their way through the bricks.
"Their bedroom is closed to you."

One brick, two bricks, three bricks, four.

She reaches from •a••y's jacket to her pencils
an• the portrait of herself.
The arms an• legs are •ifficult to get right,
the feet even more so.

"You foun• her clothes all over the living room that morning."

God is dog backwards so she writes them both
till she smells daddy's dinner,
steak with mustard and Bordeaux in the jus.
At the table, the meat glistens
like her cheeks in the candle light.

Godot whispers sweetly now,
"You'll never be loved."

She hears it in that corner
by the charcoal sketch.

9

She emerges from the fig trees by the sea. Ailis is curled in her arms but they are not her arms. When the baby feeds at her breasts, it is beautiful but they are not her breasts. Her clothing pulled back and every line exposed. She's the eternal female rising—not a Botticelli, rosy in flesh, but the *Venus de Milo* unearthed in stone, polished and without breath. The sensuality of nature has captured her but nature and she are divorced. She floats above it and herself. The sea around is still as glass where she beholds her reflection. She is transforming into landscapes—her eyes the shallow far off sea and her hair grown red especially down there, like the copper soil. The mother and child physical bond melts them but her mind watches the scene like a postcard she is not part of.

It's July in Greece but no one is ever on the beach except the man on horse riding bareback distant along the shore. The blonde Swede worn from the sun who will never leave. They wade into the water, mother and child. Maebh could just lay the baby on the sand but the baby is part of her body still and if she sets the baby down it might push off like faded paper. Waxy leaves float on the water. She walks along the horizon hip-high in water for some time. Then she pulls Ailis's head up to face hers and dunks down into the water up to her shoulders. She squints in the sun and Ailis's little scraggly body twists into her and coos. She leaves the water and heads back up the cliff through the orchards to the house, a bit of lunch and an afternoon nap. She has discovered day lounging in shade and out and about breezy nights on bare arms and legs.

JC and she have come to the Peloponnese, somewhere south of Sparta, near a little hamlet called Molai. Chris and Elsa are renting their apartment in Paris for the summer and with that money, government baby allowance and maternity leave, they buy plane tickets. They rent a derelict farmhouse with sheets hanging in place of the door and tiny windows to keep the bugs out. The thick stone-walls protect them from the sun but there's no electricity and the farmer brings them containers of water every few days.

Ailis holds in tight and Maebh swaps a black fly away just as it stings her thigh. She hikes back up wondering why there is not a soul to be seen from here but the faint line of trees in the groves above, well pruned and spaced, to remind that despite everything this is not a wilderness. You walk easy in the shade, admiring the fruits hanging in various stages of ripeness from the branches.

Maebh spies JC through the trees at his painting just under the front awning. She walks past his crouched back, the patches of burn and darkened oily skin. He wears nothing but a pair of greyed boxer shorts these days. They were black when they first arrived—he, too, is mellowing into the landscape and as quietly as Maebh. He thinks more than he works like her. She adds that to the list she has in her mind of things they have in common and goes into their little hovel to put Ailis down for a nap. The urge to sleep with her baby in her arms is strong and most days she does, but today there's a bunch of laundry.

She drags out a big flat bin and fills it with water which should be hot enough in the sunlight to wash things in a few hours. Then she goes back in to sort through the dirty clothes and JC follows her to make another '*putain •e café*', cursing at the fireplace which functions well over by the far end without overheating the place and remains immune to the large grill that gets thrown at it at least once a day.

"You freshwater girls piss me off," he says throwing a fig at her and grabbing some twigs and larger branches.

"This fig is like an introverted pink flower—just like me," she says, biting into it. It's thick and seedy in texture and more nourishing than thirst quenching.

"*Bordel de chiotte*!" JC says in exasperation as he hacks with that rusty axe with rather more dexterity and muscle than you'd expect. There is a cigarette in his mouth and his eyes don't even seem open. Sure he has scratches but all his limbs are intact.

"Can you collect some more figs for lunch?" he asks.

"Ok!" she says wondering what masterpiece he will cook next. He doesn't like eating the same thing twice. She picks the figs from four different trees, walking about in circles around them, looking for those that are mostly dark purple with still a bit of green. They hang at arm's length, pluckable without strain but the farming secrets which made that possible must have been hard earned. She bends down also to collect some scraps of rough curled bark for the fire, admiring the thin layers of lighter skin underneath. There are olive trees in the orchard, too, with a lighter green leaf and tiny knots of olives. Maebh wishes they could stay to watch them bloom in all their colours. In fact, she wishes she could stay in this idyllic spot forever.

Nature and man are well balanced in these lands and it is easy to see how art and philosophy peaked here some 2500 years ago. The erotic, which maternity has more heightened than lulled in Maebh, thrived here also, as she comes upon herself stretched out vulnerable like a Camille Corot nude and then she feels herself running like Daphne with tangled limbs. Some sculpted lust has her by the throat and she is hatched in desire, eternal as time.

"Where's the spade?" she asks handing JC a cradle of bark and twelve figs of about the same tenderness.

"I have no idea."

She heads down, with a bit of paper, but without the spade—already lost—to the ravine which is their toilet. She almost forgets to make sure no one is around when there never is and crouches between the long grasses and wildflowers. You can see the sea ahead and there are forest fires lining the far hills red—all is framed in primary colours. She might be far from flush toilets but is resigned to any struggle with the physical world in this little spot. She stands up and kicks a good few showers of earth over the perfect coiled little pile with paper she's left behind. This holiday has been good for their digestion.

She finds the spade beside another better smoothed pile where one of them must have left it. Back at the house she places the spade at the side of the house and scoops a jug full of warmed water from the bin over her hands.

"You Canadians love your camping," JC says as she dries her hands on her dress.

"I've never been camping."

They couldn't get through a winter living like this but for city folk are managing well so far, in summer. Maebh picks up her book to maybe read a little under the awning with JC out front painting again. As long as there's time to read they are not savage. Maebh has somehow managed to read a few chapters already but is not reading the way she was while pregnant.

"Are you still on nineteenth-century stuff?" JC asks.

"I'll never forgive Dickens for killing off Nancy."

"I told you to read more Flaubert."

"Loved it!"

"And Balzac?"

"Too cruel!"

"What book is that then?" he says.

"*The Birth Of Tragedy.*"

"Nietzsche? Pffouf!"

He's scrawling camouflage stones again—ochre, one and two—onto large pieces of white paper he has held down at the corners with some logs he found out front. She wishes she knew how to ask him why he is painting a bunch of stones but they've been clucking back and forth long enough. So she starts talking about the Nietzsche.

"There is a didactic pull in Euripides which takes away somehow from the theatre of it. Crowds on stage are more realistic but the characters are less symbolic in a poetic way of complex life experience."

JC looks up for a second as if she might have said something but then shakes his head in amusement.

"*N'importe quoi!*"

He pours a few drops of Retsina into one of the glasses lying around that they haven't broken and tops it with water. "I think you need some Bacchus, Madame Philosophe," he smiles handing it to her.

She withdraws into the wine sip, sip warm with green winds admiring and forgetting what it might taste like with an ice cube and how thirsty she is for large conversations.

"Lunch time," he says. *"J'ai faim."*

They move inside and over to the huge fireplace which covers the whole back wall of the house. He prepares the fire with a few of those fig and olive branches and then spreads scrunched up figs on the flat bit of dough he made earlier. Maebh sprinkles the pink seedy fruit with olive oil and he adds some feta cheese and a bit of honey.

"So pretty!"

He lays it and the pan cradled somehow on the dimmed flames. Then he grabs the yellow broom they bought the other day and starts sweeping out the place.

"I hate that American you drink with," Maebh says picking up Ailis's dirty clothes to throw in the tub outside.

"Why?"

His wife's soft body fled of shape and any spark or mineral—washing, cooking, feeding babies ad infinitum—no stove, washing machine or dishwasher—and her only daughter worn the same while her brothers stare up at father hippie long beard round the fire-pit pontificating anti-consumerism. Mother and daughter with dismayed angel grey faces but this is the land of milk and honey for father and boys satiated with the comfort of being served. A harem almost makes sense in this type of situation - fewer pregnancies for each woman and more female hands to do things. Or the men could just help out.

"Run!" - Maebh had willed this thought in her direction the one time she had joined JC at their camp and "take your daughter too."

"His wife is his slave," Maebh says.

"So, I'm not always an asshole," he says.

"Only most of the time."

"Fig pizza," he says. "Figs with toast, on pork chops, in salads. I am a genius with figs."

Maebh soaks the clothes with tons of shampoo. It was that or dishwashing liquid. She sifts the silk creamy bubbles evenly throughout but they will never get clean. Then she sets the table just outside the front door under the awning which is only really a bunch of branches but it does give shade. Maebh enjoys not having Ailis in her arms but does feel as if she's missing something. She might cling to her daughter too much but as she lays the knives and forks between the chipped blue plates, she thinks about Nietzsche, Greek Tragedy and Medea rising up like a banshee - stabbing her own children or maybe strangling them with her bare hands. Maebh thinks about Nora in *The Doll's House* closing the door on her children. Ibsen gets it better than Euripides, she thinks, knowing some dulled part of her understands both plays better than she can explain however much she loves her daughter.

She adds a twist top bottle of retsina to the table and cuts a few slices of saucisson and tomato that she finds hidden at the back of the pantry. There's a sprig of mint too which she thinks might be nice so she adds it to the plate.

JC brings the pizza over. He places it pan and all on the rickety wooden table obviously happy with his handiwork. He drizzles olive oil over everything, cuts the pizza into small thin slices and arranges a few of them on her plate. He adds "ah du menthe" with a flourish and a scoop of feta.

"*Et voilà*!" he says putting it delicately in front of her.

"So pretty!" she says again. She drips a bit more honey on the pizza and a bit of salt and takes a bite. "It's delicious!" And JC beams.

"The pastry is stiff."

"It's chewable."

"You must have some wine. This is a new bottle I found," he says pouring her a glass half full.

"Half that, please, and can you top it up with some water." He knocks back most of the glass with a chug and passes it to her.

"No water," he says. "It's perfect as is."

"You're in a good mood," she says.

"You finally put Ailis down," he says.

Pale green yellow, again warmer than ideal—the wine slaps the senses—lovely with the pizza, oil and mint.

They notice the flies zig and zag across the table when they put their knives and forks down and JC starts killing them the way the old men taught him to down at the bar.

"You put your hands like this on either side of the fly about three inches up and then you clap them together. Baf!" he says. "Flies can't see from the side and fly straight up into your hands."

"It's disgusting!" she says as he scrapes the dead ones off his palms and flicks them away but she can't help laughing.

She leans back in the chair reaching out her arms. The blues overhead and the clouds holding them in place. Things have been let be here but the old order still comes through and there is something about the neglect, the waywardness which comforts. Laziness and possibility often go hand in hand with hopefully a new way of viewing things that doesn't completely brush over the past.

"There's something missing," JC says staring at his empty plate. "Let's try those ugly little oranges?" He goes into the house to get them and places a few on the table.

Maebh is feeling lighter and by the time she has finished peeling one of the oranges, she's had a few sips of wine more than she should and forgotten she has a baby at all. She piles the peelings, green and brownish yellow, into a tidy bundle. Is it even an orange?

"Nico gives us oranges for free," says JC, "why ever did you buy these?" And then he juggles them—a one, two, three.

"They are a rare Turkish breed you can't find anywhere else in Greece," she says. She does feel dumb having ordered them—their stickiness all over her and they have run up credit at the grocery store for weeks already waiting for a cheque from Chris and Elsa.

"You are so gullible!" he says.

"Probably!" she says passing him a few hacked up looking slices. The fruit peel was thin and hard to peel and dripped all over the place.

"*Putaine*, they are good!"

The orange refuses to separate in expected sections as she pulled it apart and in the mouth it's as if all the pulp has dissolved in juice, sweet and surprising. And then because oranges remind her of that summer with Maxim, Maebh wonders what else she might pull apart—what else might be better than it actually appears. Their marriage perhaps?

"We get along so well on holiday," she says.

JC looks at her in a way he hasn't in a long time.

"Oh Maeeeeeeeeebh, would you take off your dress for me?"

So she does shift out of the dress and after that the both of them shy for a moment as she sits there in her black lace underwear—a bit worn grey now too like JC's. She wears it every day almost and even swims in it but feels it tracing her skin like when she first bought it and she blushes like the sliced tomato they forgot to eat, hoping he'll ask her over to him but enjoying the space between them and wondering if they can't right here and now find the intimacy they've never found.

She stands up wanting him to look at her more and then, because she doesn't know exactly what else to do, wanders inside to get a bottle of sparkling water she left somewhere. She catches a look at herself in the little mirror that hangs by the door. She is parched and enjoys feeling his eyes on her—she walks like she doesn't notice this though in an act so practised since childhood it is second nature.

"Is that my wife?" JC had asked her soft post baby paunch the first day they arrived.

But that is mostly gone now and Maebh rather enjoys the lingering maternal softness. She looks at the work clothes she has hanging there in case, by some fluke, she gets a teaching job here and they end up not going back to Paris. Actually, they even bought one way tickets—some itinerancy pulling her and everything she owns from country to country. But she never wears these clothes. She does put a bit of lipstick on, which is something you are not supposed to need in the middle of nowhere. Not too much, she prunes as the fig trees and removes most so it seems natural—just a little brings light to her face.

JC eyes her still and then pulls out the clarinet he bought in Paris just before Ailis was born, for a little afternoon serenade.

"Woody Allen taught himself clarinet. He has a band in New York," he says.

"Somehow you do manage to get a good sound of it," she says.

He grins proud of himself and she's not lying. He plays on and she meets his eyes. But just as she must slip onto his lap—and she has often felt as much at other odd times across tables when wine and conversation can-can and sex is closeness and the journey in itself of the day and not something fit in around toothpaste—JC starts fussing with his reed and she's gone to him. He puts the clarinet to his mouth with greater concentration and minstrels about. The sounds bitter, wild and lonely. He too is moved but not really with her.

Her glass has one last drop of wine left and she tilts it in the sun a little to make it sparkle more as if to shed with it a comeback tear but he's far away. And he has always been so indifferent when she wanted him most. She has tried to explain but he brushes it off.

Ailis wakes with her little cries and all wants beside the maternal are stilled with, unfortunately, a touch of anxiety and resentment. And for a minute also, she had thought that if only neither of them had to work, if only they were independently wealthy, they could find passion and continue on quite happily together.

She picks up Ailis and coos over her but silently—eye to eye bluer and fairer skinned than any of them expected given JC's pale olive skin that tans deep brown, almost black, and his darker hair and eyes. She drinks a bunch of water and eats more pizza to drown the wine. "I only really had two small quarter glasses", she reflects. "It should be fine!" Ailis's head is bobbing back and forth on her, looking to feed till she sits with her on the wonky sleeping structure. Ailis nestles into latch position, the same smile, gulping as she did the first night her cries woke like a slap in the face. Maebh had been indignant the nurse hadn't come but with some instinct had lifted her from the crib and unbuttoned her nighty. Ailis had almost jumped finding the nipple straight with a lust for life that she had seemingly figured out after one feeding. Now, her lips pierce a little gorgeous the breast that had almost started to milk of itself in anticipation. Maebh has time to read but watches her child's littleness instead while the hormones she knows she must fight to birth child after child after child, pierce her heart.

Ailis had come out cooing wide, so curious, with mouth pursed up, sucking in the world she saw around her. "She must be tired. Put her in her crib!" the nurse had suggested but this child was delighted with life.

The day of her birth, Maebh had woken late around ten feeling something like period pains come and go.

"It's weird but I think they are coming in every ten minutes." Weird because she was rolling in a kind of fog clock ticks didn't seem in step with.

"Don't be silly!" JC said. "The due date is a week away."

Then she went to the bathroom and wiped away a liquid thicker than water.

"Do you think that was my water breaking?"

"No! No! You'd have a puddle at your feet and you would be screaming."

"It hurts though."

"Where's my tweed blazer?"

People start running at this type of news but JC had a lunch appointment he was looking forward to and Maebh absent-mindedly passed him the blazer she always knew where to find.

"I don't think you should leave," she said when he closed the door.

She called the clinic. She had sense enough for that but has somehow in the fuzz decided that this was not it but some false alarm.

"Yes, do come in but don't rush. Take your time!"

So Maebh took her time—"I'll go in for a visit," she said aloud. Djamila was over in five though. Maebh wasn't expecting that either.

"It's okay!" Maebh said.

"I brought you ice cream," Djamila said. She was out of breath and Maebh ate some though it tasted too sweet while they walked over to the taxi stand in Place Clichy, stopping every once in a while—friction pulling everywhere, with the pains.

The taxi driver kept looking back relieved she was quiet and vertical.

"But I really don't think I'm anywhere near ready to give birth. It is too early and the pain is not unbearable!" she told Djamila.

At the hospital, they told her to change and wait in the waiting room.

"Change?" she asked.

"Where is your bag?"

"What bag?"

So she lay on the delivery table in her blue flowered dress till the nurse took the dress off to connect her to the monitor. She was a bit cool and they didn't offer to cover her with a sheet or anything. And she is not good at asking for things so she gave birth stark naked. They did ask if she wanted an epidural though and were relieved she said yes. She had thought about trying without, but JC was so curious, when he eventually arrived, to see every little detail of the cutting, poking, pulling and stitching he forgot to hold her hand. He seemed to be peering right through her open and shaved vagina all the way up the birth canal. He stood there in his light blue shirt, dark hair swept back from his forehead, his thumb and forefinger on his chin and then he would rush off right after with her chequebook to get clothes for them and buy diapers and drinks at the bar.

Maebh had just wanted to close her eyes.

"Push, a little!" they said.

"I can't feel anything!"

Then they tickled her feet and she laughed and Ailis was born on her own, with no push and on Maebh's tummy, curled up in odd little stripes of red goo. Pummelled full of oxytocin, the physical part of birth had been easy, too easy. Maebh hadn't even suffered—except for those metal stitches and the sign JC wrote for his daughter when they got home—'Welcome Home Ailis'.

"I love her more than you now!" he had said.

Maebh is starting to fall asleep when she hears JC outside the house putting his clarinet back in its case. Then he starts insulting his painting. Ailis is pulling her breast too much so Maebh shifts her to feed on the other side. She then sees something move into her frame of vision. A black creature, tail standing straight up behind it, scuttles across the floor. Maebh curls her legs tighter and throws the damn Nietzsche at it hard. The scorpions are poisonous here and they are a good walk from Molai and the hospital is even farther. She looks at the book lying there knowing she has likely not killed it and that she is an absolute fool for coming here with an infant and half a husband. "JC!" she tries to scream but doesn't. She leans her head against the cold wall of the house. Being here is a flight from reality and a flight of madness, too, but she can feel the salts of the Mediterranean sea, the swaying mass of it running out past Italy and France, Egypt and Tunisia. The basin of humanity is here, man muck shifting history. She has craved the feel of this her whole life. Ailis, Nietzsche and scorpion—at breast, at hand and underfoot. And her brain just hasn't been functioning rationally for some time.

"Let's walk into town?" JC says peeking in.

'At least he still seeks her company,' she thinks.

They walk the thirty minutes most days into Molai for groceries and sometimes they stay for dinner till late. There's not much there but a small supermarket and a souvlaki place with decrepit blue painted furniture run by a woman, swollen saggy legged and decrepit too. They walk home by the silhouette of the shepherd at his staff like a lamppost to see who will go by. They lost the baby carrier hitch hiking last week but Maebh carries Ailis in her arms for long periods, and even as she gets bigger—the muscles seem to develop to accommodate her.

That evening JC is drunker than usual, singing and falling all over the street. Maebh is afraid he might get hit by the few stray cars going by or pass out in the ditch so they decide to hitchhike as a truck passes and it stops right away. The man seems very happy to drive them and urges her with a flourish into the front seat beside him and then his young son gets in on the other side blocking her in the middle. The men in Greece have typically paid no attention to her so she is off her guard. Or at least this is how she chastises herself after it seems they would throw her, baby and all to the road for a good romp. Maebh plays it cool squished as she is between the eyes of them on her.

"*Au secours*! Save me, Maebh!" JC hollers from the back of the truck, arms and legs flying about in air, as she talks to them.

"My husband and I are staying here for the summer. He's a painter."

And then to herself as the father starts groping her, "No don't pinch my breast. It's not yours actually. My daughter is just born and it's not mine either." With Ailis in her arms she moves her body away from the upper arms the father rubs against her as he drives. She leans towards the son a bit more. He seems lustier than his father but not as immune to a scolding. Don't be ridiculous, her eyes say. Fucking a woman with a baby won't be interesting and she tries to appear bored, anything but afraid.

"Yes, just drop my husband and I off here please," Maebh says finding her firm voice and then louder. "Stop now and thank you!"

They seem to be pulling over.

"We walk from here," she says relieved that somehow it seems to have worked or maybe they got what they wanted. Or maybe JC's hollering does save her. Maebh couldn't scream for the scorpion and can't here either.

"Go home to the woman one of you calls wife and the other mother," she mutters when she feels her feet touch down on the side of the road, looking back at them in warning. She likes to think she somehow had it in her to protect herself but they are no longer looking her way.

JC scrambles out supplicating. He lands by the road with a thud and rolls into the grass.

"My legs are broken!" he says kicking them up and down so loud Maebh can't hear herself.

"Help me up!" he says. So she does.

She opens her mouth to explain but knows she and her experience are not seen to him and she buries them with everything else.

The night landscapes wash them away as soon as they step forward and the truck lights pass. The pale blue shadow of the full moon overtakes the grove in a wide gorgeous gust and the trees wave turquoise in their seabed. They move towards the house in this thickness and soon drunk as JC in the jello air, up is down in the moonbeams and their limbs wave like fish. They stand still a moment to stare at the miracle moon. A lush, lush aperture high and round just to the left, all present, all forgetting.

They will take the boat across to Brindisi next week. Shady on one side and sun-filled on the other—a pool filled with bathing bodies that disgusts after the quiet of their beach.

"Plane tickets are much more expensive from here," the agent will tell them. "You can hitch-hike up to France with someone you meet on the boat."

Hitch-hike!—Maebh won't even blink. How the moon blues transcend and then they are home.

10

It's a flat in the white house on the Malone Roa• in south Belfast.
She kneels arms outstretched in that small bedroom at night,
She prays but the halo light through the tiny skylight above her bed does not comfort.

She's seven an• Sinea• is five.
There are apples in the tree outside
they play games with on Halloween.

She stan••s face turne• to the tree,
Too well hi••en in her fox costume so her cousins walk right past.
She has become the tree.
Or maybe she hasn't un•erstoo• that the fun is in getting caught.

They are on their own here without dad.

In the house on the cobble-stoned street in Cabbagetown,
Mum wrote, "FUCK YOU CAL"
in thick burgundy paint on the wall up the stairwell.

They lose him an• that house in front of the park,
the tobogganing hill and the close-cropped greens
that le• twenty minutes un•er the Don Valley Parkway
to the outdoor swimming pool.

"Your father never bore• me Maebh," Mummy sai•.
"He's just too much!"

11

It is after midnight and JC is listening to Steve Reich's *The Train.*

"Le train, le train!" he sings while his body mimes out fiendish chugga-chugga mechanics. The street shadows that normally comfort slash across the room and the windows move past dim landscapes.

"I'm a Jew!" he says.

"Nice try!" Maebh says.

"Les fascistes, get me off this train."

"What train?"

She wants off too. There are red spots under her eyes. She coughs up green phlegm into tissues strewn about the place. Her back is stomped down with knots and aches and the night talks to her. JC blames her, which is convenient as she blames herself. She stepped away from their union long ago but their failed marriage is only part of the problem. The other parts she heaps ruthlessly upon herself. She might be more sympathetic to JC than he is to her but views the source of their mutual suffering through faded lenses no better. Her self-loathing mocks inner weakness while his curses the outer circumstances which refuse to indulge him. He found someone to pay the bills and is angry that someone, her, is doing such a bad job of it. She had never really expected anything from him in the first place but believed too much in her ability to sustain them and this is a kind of hubris or naiveté. The supposition being, if you expect nothing from your lover he can't hurt you but that hadn't come true. It's a muddled up equation where the self-destruction she allows pretends to a self-awareness she controls and how 'survive' becomes the question over how to live. Living means fulfilment and understanding and nice couches and that's harder than how educated people like her hide behind finding money to pay the rent.

Ailis is ten months old, still nursing and sleeping beside her on the bed. But Maebh sleeps only in fits between night feeds, her thoughts and JC.

One hour ago round midnight, it was JC careening up the stairwell with groceries that would have been nice to have had hours ago. He banged on the door because he was so drunk he couldn't see the keyhole. Not that he needed to, Maebh had heard him stumbling on the stairs as soon as he entered the building. She opened the door right away as he fell flat on his face.

"Ah, Maebh I walked all over Paris, back and forth from Opéra to Place Clichy ten times but I couldn't find you!" He looked lonely as she took off his coat and set him up on the couch.

"Are you hungry?" she asked.

"I just want you to have a drink with me," he said. "You never come out anymore."

"I can't!"

"You are such a drag!"

"I know!" She puts the groceries in the fridge. Potatoes, some *chèvre*, a lettuce. She placed some of the clementines he had just bought in a bowl on the coffee table beside him and some bread and *jambon*, too—quick, efficient. She was not being caring but rather hoping some food would sober him. He was staring dark into the abyss, an empty champagne glass in one hand and an unlit cigarette in the other. She saw and had never seen any understanding of his part in their suffering in this stare. His demands are all of others and this is something, because hers are all of herself and that she does secretly admire.

"There isn't a drop in the house!" he said.

"Maybe you have had enough," she said. "We have a child which requires more of a lifestyle change than anyone tells you."

His eyes flashed out accusation—black, more alone than ever but then so was she, arms in deep at her chest.

It's the only thing to do since Languainc folded and she lost her job. The owners had written off all their housing, travelling and food costs on company dime and the rip-off had trickled all the way down the chain. Maebh had even taken home a phone that never worked on the last day when everyone was clearing out their offices.

In fact, losing the job brought some relief. She did get headhunted by another company but could not get out of bed for the interview. They will live for a year on the severance pay when it finally arrives and some financial assistance from the town hall. Her step too light when she went to pick it up and she'd made rather too much of an effort to look nice.

"They are giving money to top models now," an old man had said in the line behind her—'*l'accent populaire*' in his voice.

"I lost my job!" she had said, wishing she had Ailis on her hip.

"But you have a rich husband."

People often think that. She had swung by him quickly, embarrassed by the chunk of bills in her hand. It was enough for three months rent past due. Their situation had only improved for a short time but she knew that it was not something she could compare to the desperation of others who have lived in poverty for generations without help from town hall. This job loss does not frame who she is but is like an experiment someone like her with an education and middle-class demeanour can pass through. She wonders if a sense of middle-class guilt hadn't allowed this self-neglect to happen or if she was in denial of how even hundreds of years after *Tess of the D'Urbervilles* having a child with the wrong man could wreck your life.

"Why is Ailis still waking up like a newborn?" a mum of three at work had asked her.

"I can't bear tears!" Maebh had said starring with amazement at the line of perfect blue eyeliner round her colleagues bright eyes.

"Put her on the bottle—you're skin and bones."

"I don't know how!"

"And why don't you put her in *crèche*?"

Maebh can't imagine Ailis with strangers, other snotty-nosed babies, pre-prepared foods, left alone.

"At least you stopped going home for lunch to feed her."

Maebh had taken the metro a few stops north, opened her blouse with one hand, scarfed down cold stew with the other and headed back down to teach again every lunch hour for months when Ailis was still an infant.

"Yes, JC put her on solids."

He makes her food himself from scratch and Maebh is impressed and relieved. Mami might have suggested it but JC has carried it out well enough. Ailis had been slumped over her father's shoulder helplessly sobbing, those first few days back to work and whenever Maebh looked back, she was wracked sick that JC hadn't just walked out on her or even throttled her. But now, Ailis is trotting around the furniture to the windows where she stares out long at the birds over the trees behind the cemetery walls.

"We should all work three days." Maebh had said. "It would help create jobs for the unemployed and give both parents a chance to make a living, pursue hobbies and stay at home with the kids."

"Executives could never split up their hours," she had said.

"Why not—they work too much and others not enough!"

"My husband wouldn't even consider it."

"How are women ever going to make themselves heard. Five thousand years of culture and we are still nothing!" Maebh had said.

"It'd be so much easier to stay home, though."

"We will never get a chance to share what we have to share," her voice had gripped. She feels her whole self scrunched down by women's invisibility in history.

"Maybe child-rearing is what we have to share?"

"No!"

"You don't have to be so fascist about it!" she had said.

Dads wiping down the kitchen sink and mothers breaking the glass ceiling—Maebh's knuckles clenched round this mantra.

"And if the state can't allow for a system that supports families more, parents like JC and I should be handed abortion papers at their first echography."

"Maebh, how could you!"

"I love her too much for this life," she had said.

Her friend left and Maebh sat down by the *Time* cover of a starving woman from Somalia and her starving baby. The baby's eyes were shut with flies and her mouth latched on just barely to the wrinkled breast. Actually, Maebh had been staring at the magazine off and on throughout the conversation. She bent over to touch them and then rolled them up, slipping the magazine into her bag hoping the weight of it might help her move past her own puny life problems.

"There's enough food for everyone stockpiled and rotting. They just won't distribute it fairly," Dad always said.

Some essential memory of the Irish famines—people crawling into hovels and wrapping skeletal arms around each other to die—haunts his eyes and hers as well no doubt. Maebh had taken the magazine out again and put it back on the office side table. It was too heavy and she was not doing anything to help, hardly able to put one foot in front of the other.

"I am part of the problem!" she thought. "Humanity has debased itself at every level of the food chain."

She headed soft down the red carpet stairs away from it and past the lower end stores on the Chaussée D'Antin. At Trinité, she opened the garden gate and felt words composing in her mind amidst the trees and fountains. The starving mother and child, the too-bright flower beds and someone over-feeding the pigeons stale bread. The sun was setting from left to right pale mauve while she sat there too stricken to move.

But maternity is not the only challenge, Maebh thinks coming back to the hellish night as JC starts his cacophonic eulogy to Steve Reich again.

"*Los Bastar•os!*" he says.

Maebh leans up on her elbow and just sees him through the night shadows splayed out on the floor banging his fists against the floor.

"You look ridiculous!" she says.

He always speaks Spanish when he gets revolutionary but she can't imagine what existential angst has afflicted him. 'I'm an asshole' might be a better refrain. She can say that he is making an acceptable if melodramatic attempt at expression.

"I'm turning the music off JC. It's not helping!"

He stands guard by the stereo but her patience is wearing.

"Please, JC, I need to sleep!"

"That's all you ever do!"

"I know!" she says again instead of it's late and sleep is what people do. But she hates coming off status quo and then she starts off on a coughing fit that rips her chest out of itself. She is rotting and hacking particles from the inside out. She reaches for the box of tissues. It's empty so she feels for some dried up ones by the bed.

JC picks up a bunch of clementines. He juggles them first rather badly and then because they won't circulate as they should, he throws them one by one hard against the wall. Maebh rolls over as small as she can. But then he throws another one right at her.

"What the hell JC!"

He laughs a nasty laugh.

"I need to paint," he says turning the lights on full blast and grabbing his brushes. There are clementines all over the apartment—juices splash the wall.

"Can't you continue your Jackson Pollock in the morning," she says.

"No, I can't! I need a studio!"

"Well get a job to pay for one," she says.

JC looks at her with that pointed look.

"You are just like my parents," he says playing on her nurturing side.

"No, I'm not!" she says instead of 'maybe they are right', so he succeeds.

"I'm an artist!" he says.

"Art is a privilege!"

"It's a necessity!"

Maebh laughs at this cliché as her eyes find the Elias Canetti book and the journal she hasn't touched in months. *Crowds and Power*—the title had grabbed her when she saw it on the shelf at her parent's house in Ireland at Christmas. She hasn't been the woman who put these things neatly in a pile by the window for months, either, but still remembers the last time she had had a thought.

How she had moved through the metro wondering at Canetti's theories. He said people sat at opposite ends of the train-cars from strangers because they feared each other and that the larger and tighter the crowd grew the more these fears dissipated till an individual allowed another to graze gently past shoulder to shoulder. But she had wondered instead, her mind buzzing with the joy of words, as she walked through the park past the birds flying so perfectly over the trees, if it wasn't an innate sense of harmony that had people put themselves next to each other with appropriate distance—that nature has a kind of essential quest for harmony and that people are born with a sense of respect for each other's personal space and a sense of how to position themselves best within it. That much as we seem to destroy each other, we do want the other to exist.

Maebh can't recall any of that now or even imagine a word such as harmony exists but the sight of the books calms her and one day she'll get back to them.

But JC is looming over Maebh wailing—"art is a necessity!"

He sits down beside her way too close, she thinks, recoiling, and he kicks off the 700F British brogues his mother bought him. Maebh is a bit afraid of this ugly outburst—it's worse than usual but she's angry too.

"And the fancy shoes you couldn't live without," she shouts after him as he gets up to head to the bathroom, "are they a necessity?"

JC's mother can always be counted on for grooming expenditures come his birthday. And the only time Maebh has ever seen his mother truly disgusted with him was when he badly needed a haircut.

"Even artists need to pay for themselves."

"Pay! Pay!" he says. And then he starts throwing the clementines against the windows which rattle terribly so she gets up to remove them from him and puts them in the kitchen.

She might have respected him more if he had been upfront about his inability to make money from the beginning but then the signs had been there and he probably had in his way.

"Aren't you the angel martyr," he says. His voice indulgent, mischievous as if he read her mind. Maebh is tired of fighting now. She sucks miserably on the clementine. Her whole self has turned into one of those Russian dolls which holds many other placid replicas of itself, one inside the other until they are too tiny to see.

"Come to bed," she says turning off the lights.

She's nauseous and when she sinks into the mattress which they didn't find on the street but came with the apartment and is quite good quality—she wishes she could keep on sinking and sinking.

JC crawls out on the balcony. He careens in the moonlight and steps up onto the little chair hanging too far over the railing which used to terrify her because he doesn't have the best balance. "*Bordel de merde*," she hears him say amidst the slipping of his feet on the chair. He fell off a fifth floor balcony at one point, the story goes, onto a Volkswagen beetle—totalling the car but without breaking a bone. He's crawled out onto the roof though so many times and bragged to friends about how her pretty tears begged him to come in that Maebh no longer cares.

"I like you better now that you love me less," he says falling into the room. She's relieved that ignoring his tryst with held breath has worked.

"You reap what you sow," she says.

Her love was supposed to erase nascent pain and provide everything he couldn't provide for himself. She had wanted it to. The question is why she caters to it so and why she doesn't expect the same from him in return.

And then he throws something else at her—hard—whack on the forehead. It bounces and lands somewhere beside her. She screams a little muffled scream and Ailis wakes up and all of a sudden JC is crawling on the floor, belly down, fists raised to wartime demons. Something is running down around her eyebrow and when she puts her hand there to wipe it more just keeps coming. Was it an accident or did the wimpy one time tennis prodigy actually have some aim?

"*Le train, le train. Sauve-moi*!" he says but his voice sounds tiny and drained.

The Steve Reich had stopped playing ages ago but the melody is ingrained in his head. Maebh says nothing, quiet as glass, to pretend she isn't there as JC drags himself slowly up the floor towards her. He's laughing slightly,

'Ha ha! The fear in your voice Maebh."

Then he just stops as if he has forgotten she is there. He swears a bit kicking his feet up and down and passes out.

Maebh feels for more of the dried up tissues with her left hand while Ailis nurses. She holds a bunch of tissues from various coughing fits to her forehead watching warily JC's jagged grey stretched out form. She might not even be the enemy just the only one in his way. She curls her feet in tight, noticing as a passing car light fills the room how his left arm almost made it to the bed.

She nurses Ailis a little, holding her close with one hand and pats at her own head which seems to be throbbing with the other. What did he hit her with? She reaches round her a bit further and finds the champagne flute nestled in the pillows—empty and unchipped. Later, there will be a perfectly marked crescent moon on her forehead. Now, the realization of how it could have hurt Ailis lying there just on the other side of her means she has to get out. Still it takes some effort, especially as she knows JC will remember none of this tomorrow and the giant polar bears of her childhood nightmares have found her and she would rather disappear.

She half trips over the Canetti, stumbling about in the shadows for the phone—war is everywhere she thinks. She calls Chris and Elsa, forgetting they're away and then she remembers that she has family in town. Her sister Roisin is here on her Erasmus year and she answers with a gurgling sweet sleepy voice that reassures.

"Sure, I'll open up the clic-clack for you," Roisin says.

They, Roisin and her boyfriend—perhaps the two tallest people in the city—live in Le Marais, in a space only slightly larger than the loft bed they have and it's going to be cramped on the pull-out thing just below them.

She wraps Ailis up and carries her and a small bag of things and they head down the stairs. If there were more stairs down Maebh would have taken them—down down looking for a bunker. She left JC stiff and neglected above—a Giacometti sculpture knocked over on the studio floor. A year ago, she would have covered him with a blanket and pulled him over somehow to the mattress.

Maebh knows she should ask him to leave but he wouldn't. She could see him crash-landing on the door at all hours and smashing windows and things. She would have to disappear if she left him but then she wasn't even sure how to handle life without him. Not yet and not with a small child alone in Paris. Anyway, there was something wrong with how she thought things through these days. Maybe there always had been where issues of the heart played out.

They would have that talk when she got back though. She will tell him she's taking Ailis to Ireland to live with her parents but he'll beg to come too because he's not ready to be on his own any more than she is. She will feel somehow that she can manage him and keep him calm and that he does seem to want to be tamed. And at the moment, it is better to have him than not. She really wants to live by the sea in Ireland and how can she do that alone?

"You can come," she will say. "But you can't drink!"

"Okay", he will say.

They will wander, before they leave, through Tuileries after just one glass of wine at a bar in the Latin Quarter—Ailis's tiny walking form in a white coat and striped hat that was JC's at the same age, and the Japanese tourists will take photos.

She leaves the Montmartre apartment building with a bandage over her eye and her velvet beret hung low to cover it. She puts Ailis, who is so distracted by the late night city she doesn't protest, easily in her stroller and they start walking. The stars are crisp, the air tight and there is not a soul on the street. But strange corner eyes follow her. Little nymphs and Picasso harlequin spirits cart-wheel, saloon women can-can and she wonders if she should have waited till morning to leave.

At the cab station in Place Clichy, she struggles to fold up the stroller with one hand and thankfully the driver gets out to help her with it. However, she decides not to go straight to hospital for a stitch or two. The sink had filled with Kool-Aid blood stuff when she made the mistake of turning the taps on to wash the wound and left a spotty residue. She almost kept it there for JC to think about but knew he would only laugh at how little blood there was.

Roisin won't even blink when she sees her. Their Mum has been known to appear with a bruise or two so they are used to it. The harlequins are spinning madly now—heavy made up faces peering.

In the morning, Roisin pours milk into the little red bowls of coffee and Maebh sets out the butter and jam. These are things you enjoy everywhere all over the country regardless of your circumstances. They sit scrunched under the loft bed on the fold-up couch with the oblong 50's style coffee table. Everything is perfectly renovated here but tiny and Maebh's grubby 35m2 studio feels more squalid than ever, but enormous, and she knows she can't stay with Roisin long.

"Pain Poilâne is just around the corner and they told me to wrap the bread like that," Roisin says as she helps Ailis take out the heavy scrap of it wrapped in a dishtowel.

"It's a bit hard to cut but we can just break it in pieces and dunk it in the coffee," Maebh says. And they continue like that to speak about the yellow fresh cut butter because food talk soothes when there is too much to say to say anything.

"Jean-Cristophe left hours ago to get to his shoot out by Cluny," Roisin says. Roisin has a JC of her own—JC *l'autre* as their father calls him not only because he is so the opposite of Maebh's JC but because he has early morning work ethic, something they all, except Roisin, despise. Maebh's JC is a decadent while Roisin's is new world slick. He started his own film company and has made a short film with Jean Reno from inheritance money and corporate sponsors. Roisin is quite a few years younger than he and taking French history at the Sorbonne and is his to pay for and photograph. Their situations are so different. Maebh is sadly starting to feel very far away not only from herself but also from Roisin, the person in the family she had always felt closest to.

Having a child in her lap squirming about and making a mess of the table with milk and jam everywhere isn't helping. It's a puny place with new wood kitchen, new wood Ikea furniture and old wood medieval ceiling beams. There is just nowhere to put Ailis here and then Maebh starts coughing up stuff—not too green this time and it's almost a relief to head over to the hospital.

It's grey in the courtyard outside but not raining and Ailis bounces the stroller happily over the cobbles.

They walk like this all the way in the grey Paris light but the hospital says it's too late for stitches.

"You will have a little scar for about ten years", they say, "depending on how fast you heal."

"Heal!" Maebh smiles a little. She is living as her doppelgänger and knows already that she's going home to JC right after this. It's just too tiring being anywhere else. She'll walk up along the canal past Stalingrad to Pigalle up to Montmartre. She'll share a cheese hot dog with Ailis and let her play in a few playgrounds along the way and chase after pigeons on the sidewalks. The long walk is easier than manoeuvring the stroller in the metro on her own and going home is easier than watching Roisin watch her the way she should be watching herself. And why would she drag Roisin into her mess anyway. JC will be calm now that he had his little escapade—cute, bed-ruffled and happy to see her. He won't believe any of what she describes happened and this will make it easier for Maebh to put it out of mind till she can figure out what to do.

"Why didn't you come right away and how did this happen?" the doctor chides her, more than necessary. She lies of course not knowing where to find the words to describe what happened, but this makes her look irresponsible in their eyes.

"We will have to give you a tetanus," they say. They—because the office is rather more full than it needs to be with interns. Maebh lies there on her tummy, that same old flowered dress up to her waist, tights and underwear pulled down. They prick her mercilessly on the bottom without warning and the needle sinks in deep and slow through muscle and fat.

Ailis squeals a bit and the intern with the pink clogs moves over to take her but she squeals louder. Maebh keeps her eyes on her to reassure her and takes her hand. Ailis calms down and even squeezes Maebh's finger back in support. She looks with some superiority and disgust at the doctors and Maebh feels some relief her daughter already knows who and what to trust. Maebh doesn't blame the doctors their smirks however. One is like that to those too humiliated to protest.

12

Maebh's parents sell their •ifferent houses
to fun• their wan•erings.

One year
they •rive through the Unite• States from the Appalachians
down to the cactus plains
an• then win• up the Rocky Mountains to California
and then to Mexico
The candy tastes like soap and
Mum and Dad drive all night.
Sinea• an• Maebh •rift in an• out of sleep
Fighting with each other to get a chance to lay down
Da• takes a whole roll of film.
The moon disappears ahead
and the sun rises in the car side mirror behind them.

"Time stands still when you keep moving
or at least it moves much slower.
Einstein proves that," Dad tells them.
All the •ifferent lan•scapes an• accents stan• still too
like the globe in their room.
Maebh makes it spin in her head,
the lines of longitu•e an• latitu•e
circling through country after country.

The next trip is through France and Spain in the old van
with scratche• out images of sausage
an• other col• meat pro•ucts written in German on both si•es of it.

Da• bought it at the petrol station in Belfast
They sleep in the van even.
Sinea• an• Maebh in the little loft be• over the boot.
Mum, Da• an• Da•'s mistress from Copenhagen
below in another mattress on the floor.
Da• is soft an• manly an•
the women wake up in see-through underwear every morning
their large nipples peeking through.

Sinead and Maebh play with the snails on the stone walls
after bowls of cereal with fri•ge-free milk.
Then they eat snails for •inner with garlic
at the best restaurants.

A bear•e• man eats peaches with puffs of cream
In a long flute• glass in front of them
And Maebh stares and stares
each mouthful flickering like jewels
in the yellow light.

She •oesn't finish her cassoulet
wishing she •are• ask for •esert.

But the bear•e• man or•ers it for her
She remembers his eyes.

In the warm night air,
the sight of the glass rising on the placemat
fuele• the realization that someone might know
what she wants even better than she.

An• she will spen• the rest of her life—
trusting too much the unknown—
waiting for other such miracles.
that they might have their way with her.

13

It's a beach south of Dublin, called Brittas Bay with a row of houses but no shops. It stretches out in a wide curve as far as the eye can see and they never even make it across. Sunny hues at one end, storms only half a mile away and between this kaleidoscope, sometime double rainbows stretch out high with enough fury between dark and light to incline one towards schizophrenia. The changes in scene hound your every addiction and slap when you dare to look away. No locals would brave this winter coast but the surfers in their wetsuits —jubilant, balancing-stick people hunched in the looming cruel waves.

The winds blows through and away and the soft greens cut the sandy beach to the sea. Day after week after month interminable, Maebh wishes she could say the same about a job, husband or child, but no, she's been waiting her whole life for the chance to surrender to this inexplicable surge of geography, landscape and empty time beyond anything she could ever manipulate or ignore. This thing, whatever it is, blows through her as it would have her ancestors and even though she's not that close to anyone in her extended family here, she has found a setting on this grey cliff that speaks to her like no other.

The ocean air has not made Maebh any less ill, however. Her lungs are still coated with the same white dung three different antibiotics have not cleared. She and Ailis meander down the dunes, digging heels into the clumps of grasses to the shore and while the dim chills to the bone, the place plays with the imagination as heartily as Greece. In fact, this coast bears resemblance to its warmer sister, except one feels more shiftiness than ease in the winds.

The wild grasses are taller than Ailis, now nearly two, but she makes her way through the forest of them, loving the climbs the flights of Parisian stairs trained her for. Full red cheeks burst out from the scarves and sweaters wrapped over top of her coat for warmth and her eyes, brilliant blue, tear up with the force of the gales. She braces herself and heads off almost on her own but never too far. With each determined step, Maebh can feel her analyzing the flat sands against the tumult around. She doesn't speak at all or make the usual childish sounds—Maebh's parents think her slow but two languages can impede the learning process and there is too much intelligence in her looks. Sometimes Maebh fears the sadness of her parents weighs on Ailis and regrets how useless they are at hiding this from her.

JC is sipping his whiskey already by the time they get back. He drinks only on Sunday now. That is the deal. Maebh should have come to Ireland without him but wouldn't have managed alone with a small child on this solitary coast. Some inherent fear has them stuck to each other and JC has promised to improve. Maebh recognizes her dependence and the confidence that comes from having him by her side. She might even be using him a bit and putting up with the alcoholism to compensate till she is ready to make the move.

The kitschy colours of Irish TV in the background contrast with the somber tones that spread out behind it through the window pain and Ailis sits there with her toy trains till she gets up to stare at the sheep which have jumped over the fence to nibble in their yard.

"The heat went off again," JC says, "but I wiped all the pieces and put them back together and I kicked the bitch a few times too."

He is clearly irritated and drowning in a tweedy sweater Maebh's mother knit for her father.

"Thank you!" she says and puts herself into his arms for some affection which he still seems to enjoy but never seeks out himself. They do have many moments like this and have established a kind of platonic détente together.

"Did you paint at all?" she asks him.

"I need a studio!" he says.

"It's a huge room," she says referring to the bedroom past the front porch which used to house a series of bunk beds they moved to the garage.

He shrugs and Maebh knows this means he is as creatively blocked as her and maybe even needs to be away from her as much as she should get away from him. Strangers he'd meet in bars used to be so charmed by him they'd offer up their homes for him to paint in but he has lost his spark and cutting him back on drink seems to have thrown him right off track altogether. Anyway, the nearest bar is a forty-five minutes' walk away, and off the main highway, so no spot for locals. Not that there are many people here at all in winter, which is why she likes it.

"I'm making roast pork with scalloped potatoes for Gaofei and Becky," he says.

"I'll make salad and apple pie," she says looking at her watch. "They'll be here in an hour."

He pours a glass of whiskey—Bushmills—but it's a modest glass so she tries to ignore it and how many were poured before. He often downs half to three quarters of a bottle every Sunday which she tries to tell him destroys as much as or more than wine every day did back in Paris but he doesn't listen. The rest of the week he sits sullen, stripped of purpose without booze. Sometimes, like with her father, Maebh actually prefers him drunk. There is something clownish yet refreshing in his antics that challenges both atrocity and banality with mean tongue.

He gets up to check the pork. It's still too pink he says and then he takes over the whole house singing. He loves the Bothy Band CD so much that Maebh's parents gave it to him, or maybe he procures it. He picks up Ailis—"Do you love an apple my *chérie* girl?" Maebh loves the song too but can't sing it: the lamentation of motherhood and married life with a drinker parallels her own situation and that of her parents too much.

"Oh! have a glass," he says but she shrugs. She is mindful of her health and so fatigued, caring for Ailis is about all she can muster. She heads off to make tea with honey wondering why tea does more for her than him. She has more of a preference for lucidity than he—a famous non-drinker had said that somewhere and it had stuck in Maebh's mind.

"I'm so sorry!" she says when he comes up beside her to help.

"For what?" he says.

"That we are stifling each other."

"C'est ça!"

And this confession soothes in its way. Drink loosens the tongue but for JC it's necessary as air and without it he is unfit for human interaction. Maebh thinks that if there had been more between them it might have been different but there's likely an issue he needs to face within himself that neither Maebh nor any woman could affect in any positive way.

She cuts apples and gets Ailis to shape them out with brown sugar onto the bit of pastry shell she bought at the supermarket. The sheep fields behind the house go on and on and she stares longingly out over them, admiring the way the grass puffs up in irregular clumps on the loamy fertile dark earth. Nothing is flat here and even the golf course looks more natural—less garish—than anything you might see in North America. Walking on that bouncy grass is such joy. You feel distanced, uplifted even, by the soil itself and the realities deep within the earth's core crust, and the air is gentle away from the sea. It nourishes in it's way while the rough coast pulls the life out of you and strips the skin of nutrients.

They have been here all winter and Maebh, as was the case in Greece, feels she could stay here forever. However, she only has a bit more unemployment insurance coming to her and then she will have to get back to work—teaching, again, of some kind is unfortunately all she knows how to find. She has given up hoping JC might sell a painting or find some work as well. She puts the pie in the oven wishing she could find a job out here in the country that might keep them there. Neither of them can drive, though, so even if they could afford a car it wouldn't be possible and there's not much transit. Maebh has hitchhiked a few times into Dublin and Wicklow but that's not a reliable or safe way to get to work each day.

Maebh turns to organizing the living room. She places books in a little pile at the corner of the coffee table. She is finally starting to read women writers. *Wuthering Heights* was on the shelf here beside a Maeve Binchy. Then she bought Charlotte Brontë, George

Eliot and Jane Austen at a bookshop in Dublin. Emily tackles the uncomfortableness of what it means to be human best, but all of the books are immensely readable and this eases slightly her anxiety of whether a woman can be an artist or not. It might not even be that late for her to give it a try.

"What are these toys doing all over the place again?" she says tripping over them.

She puts all of Ailis's plastic toys in the toy box but leaves out the pretty teddies and the wooden train set.

"You only tidy up for visitors," JC says.

"Well, why should our guests have to wade through our miserable shit!" she says.

She sees Gaofei and Becky pull up the lane, glad the potatoes are done and the table set.

"They're here JC," she says in warning.

He is singing way too loud and has that frantic look she knows means she should have invited them another day. She's also wishing she could sit down and hide behind another book.

"It's crispy pink, our piggy," JC says examining the roast pork in the oven. " Just like Maebh!"

Maebh puts her hand to her face and rushes over to the front mirror to dap on some powder foundation to cover up her blemished skin, but Becky catches her.

"Oh dear! You haven't put your face on yet," she says.

"Not that it makes any difference," Maebh says.

"Motherhood wrecks you a bit," Becky says so Maebh hugs her.

Maebh met Becky and a few other mothers at a La Leche League meeting. The farmer up the road told JC she might like to join. The woman who ran the event from her house let her son feed from her breasts like he was opening the fridge door.

Becky's husband, Gaofei, teaches ESL like her but not because he stumbled into it. He has a Master's degree in linguistics and now teaches at the local grammar school. They had lived in France a few years, too, before their marriage, so Maebh kisses him three times on each cheek in the French way and says, "Welcome fellow, how do you spell your name, compatriot."

"Actually, my parents call me Richard."

They seem a bit chuffed by the chance of dinner with an artist couple. Actually, people are often under various illusions about how interesting Maebh and JC are, perhaps because people want to believe themselves associated with the kind of artist couple they have decided they must be. Maebh wipes down the counter and dinner smells nice, so there is still a chance of keeping this up.

Gaofei and Becky smile at JC with pity when they see him reeling about. JC has told them Maebh hasn't had sex with him since before Ailis was born, which Maebh reasons seems to have made them think she has caused his drinking, because they don't seem to have any pity for her. Maebh coughs a little into her tissues and pours out some wine for their guests.

"Great sex is the panacea!" she says seemingly out of nowhere. "Let's drink to that but how do you get it?"

"No idea but we have three children under four so we must have gotten something right," Becky says, smiling fondly at her husband.

JC offers Gaofei a whiskey and Maebh sits down with their new baby, who is so well stuffed and gurgly, Maebh likens her to a troll. She even says that out loud, but with such tenderness that Gaofei, who is already deep red from a few sips of wine, looks at her with astonishment but forgives her. They don't over-parent them in that British way. The two older kids say hello loudly and run about with uncombed hair and food stuff on clothes and noses. Ailis watches them from her little perch by the window with perhaps a touch of disdain.

JC explains how he spent the week kicking the boiler. Gaofei and Becky sit in close comfort together, admiring his comedic talents. Maebh wonders at their happiness. She sees them in their grey-stoned cottage and the white bed which fills the main room of it. The flood of light in the space from six huge windows east, west and north is exquisite. Light flows up the linen curtains through to the rose bushes and wild toy-strewn lawn. Standing in that room, she can't imagine that they have ever made love without affection, without any sense of feeling adored by the other. If Maebh hadn't realized it before, it is in the presence of this couple that she feels her misery most. She gets up from the couch abruptly and gives the little bundle back to Becky. The child seems uncomfortable under Maebh's sad gaze and Maebh doesn't mean to taint it.

She heaps crackers on a plate with the cheese Gaofei and Becky brought and puts it on the coffee table.

"Homemade in Ireland. We bought it from a farmer in Arklow," Gaofei says cutting himself a slice.

"What happened to your other couch?" Becky asks taking the cheese knife from her husband.

"Oh a family of rats made a nest in it." JC says.

"What!"

"Yes!" Maebh says. "We were sitting on it watching TV and then one crawled out, calm as can be, nose to the ground, a monster with long sickening tail."

"How did you get rid of them?" Gaofei asks as Becky screams and shifts in her chair.

"I jumped on the dining room table with Ailis," Maebh says.

"I killed him!" says JC.

"Really?"

"With a brick to the head—paf, blood everywhere," he says.

"Is this where they got in?" Nick points to a concrete patch beside the cupboard.

"Yes!" says JC. "They ate through the fresh concrete three times till I put poison in it."

"One died in the couch and the smell was terrible," says Maebh.

"We moved it to the garage," JC says.

"They were the cutest little family when they lived in the garden shed," Maebh says.

"*A table*!" says JC.

Maebh gets up to slice the pork with the new knife they just bought, but before she gets a chance to put it on individual plates, JC has laid it out on a serving dish he had left soaking in the laundry sink with the stubborn remains of last night's trout stuck to it. He drains the dish of water with blind gaze and pours the honey carrots and onions and the juice from the pork dish all over the crispy fish skin before smacking it on the table with a bit of thyme. Maebh doesn't know what to do but sits down with the salad bowl in front of her. She mixes up the contents with the olive oil, mustard and red wine vinegar. When a few little leaves flick out onto the table, she picks them up with her fingers burning and eats them. Gaofei, Becky and JC serve themselves and start eating, but Maebh feels a bunch of phlegm rising up from her ribs, like her whole person is extricating itself from herself. She rushes off to the back room to hack it up, so glad JC has the music up a bit loud. She feels her ribs flaking paper thin against her back.

When she gets back to the table JC is chatting away about that tiny Watteau painting in the Louvre. He puts on Kurt Cobain. And Maebh still feels that leap of admiration at how he crosses from pop to classical culture so easily but now she notices that you really can see the faint traces of the fish skeleton on the serving dish.

"The worst crime is faking it!" JC says, reading from his own T-shirt. The one someone gave him or he stole. And then in the same breath,

"That Watteau, he paints the guy with a hard-on. It's a small painting but you can see it if you look carefully, there, at his trousers," he says.

Maebh wonders if she will ever again inspire a similar protrusion. The love bed of paternity seems titillation enough for Gaofei and Becky, but has brought little amorous inspiration to JC and her.

She remembers, just before the wedding, how they walked arm and arm through the Louvre's French collection on the second floor, critiquing the Corots and Lorraines.

"Idealized nature—Pfouf!"

They were nonchalantly in love that day and arrogant as though each painting was there to be destroyed for their entertainment. One falls to this temptation when the desire to produce something beautiful oneself makes itself apparent, before your own futile failure leads to an understanding of how difficult this is to fulfill.

Maebh continues coughing little dry coughs now. No one seems to notice but Ailis who pulls up on her lap to suckle like a baby. Ailis pinches her neck ruthlessly so Maebh holds her hands gently to stop her. She's still nursing and will continue to do so for another two years, once or twice a day. Maebh doesn't give her much else as a parent. She strokes the few blonde curls that are finally coming in like a halo on Ailis's head, wishing she might play or talk with the other kids. Gaofei and Becky's oldest child is sitting with a book of songs on her lap and singing a song to her younger siblings and they can all count to ten in Cantonese. Ailis can't even hum a song and only just said her first word, "Woof," last week. What kind of parents are they?

"But Maebh can't remember what a hard-on is!"JC says bringing Maebh back to the Watteau conversation.

"I'm sorry," Maebh says. "I've been tired and sick since Ailis was born," hoping that will explain why to their guests, but doesn't, without a tedious backstory.

"We were at it like rabbits all the way through pregnancies and feedings," they laugh.

Maebh had wanted him and even lay there after the birth, her whole body given to the survival of her child but wishing for some physical touch or sign of appreciation from him. She even imagined gentle looks of pride at the sight of how overwhelmingly lovely she and Ailis were together but these never came.

Gaofei and Becky seem to imagine everyone treats each other as nice as they do. JC is a most seductive character and his home alone self is usually reserved for home. One might not expect his dark side to be quite so dark. Maebh hated it that Gaofei and Becky didn't see this and tended to like JC better, perhaps because she had become such a pathetic human being. And it might be even harder to imagine that someone like her would tolerate JC's behaviour. Maebh can see Gaofei and Becky believing warm lusts end all problems. So too would Maebh's parents, and Maebh would have agreed with them a few years earlier, before the insults and objects thrown her way.

Gaofei and Becky stopped eating after the fish skeleton emerged on the platter. It didn't help matters when JC tipped it to fill his spoon with the last of the sauce after his second helping. Maebh can't move from the horror, either, not even to remove the platter from the table, but JC could care less. She admires his invincibility and might even stay with him to understand this sense of entitlement.

"Well, in China they mix fish and pork all the time, but I've never known the French to," Gaofei finally says to break the ice.

Becky who has been nursing too, finishes and passes the child to her husband who grabs the diaper bag good-humouredly to change her without being asked. He starts singing "Sing a Song of Sixpence" and all the children join in. Maebh feels she is watching 'the how to parent' video she should have watched a few years ago. She and JC have been thrown into parenting with no understanding of what it is, partly because they were, and perhaps society is too, under the assumption that it is something you just know how to do.

Gaofei walks the baby back and forth to burp her."We have to leave soon," he tells Becky.

"One for the road?" JC asks holding the whiskey bottle over his glass.

"Naw, I'm driving!" he says.

"Let me just get the dessert first."

JP is fussing with the apple pie she made earlier. He seems to be sprinkling sugar over it but Maebh worries it might be salt. She sees his tiny frame curdling over while his eyes well up, wet from the booze. He places the apple pie in the oven to give it a final toasting without turning it on and goes back to his dancing while Gaofei and Becky clap to encourage him, but then he bangs into the wall.

Maebh turns away to hide a few tears. She turns on the oven, removes the pie and brushes off the white grains of what does seem to be salt as well as she can. She adds a bit more butter and some sugar to the topping, hoping it will cancel out the salt taste and puts the pie back in the oven to melt it.

When she turns back to face the group, Gaofei and Becky have gathered up their coats and are already at the door. Three kisses on each cheek good-bye and they never see them again.

JC and Maebh watch *The Crying Game* with the TV warming like a small fire.

"The pie is delicious," he says.

"You put some salt on it," Maebh says.

"Genius!" he says.

"Yup!"

"I knew she was a he right away," JC says about the character in the film.

"I had no idea", Maebh says.

"I'd take her either way though."

"You ain't no Forest Whitaker."

"You're so mean!" he laughs.

Ailis wants to go for a walk again and JC leaps into action. Ailis is not likely to run into the waves or off the cliff but JC is too drunk to be alone with her so Maebh gets up wishing she could put the film on pause.

"You'd trust Forest with Ailis more than her own father," he says.

"And the IRA gunman," she says, "I don't want anyone calling the police on you again."

He had taken Ailis for a walk one evening by her parents' house and someone found the sight of a dark, wild-haired, staggering JC, and a straggling blonde cherub Ailis, odd enough to call the police. When the police arrived and tried to force JC into the cruiser Ailis had screamed "*Papa*" with the same French accent convincingly enough that the police had brought them home. The police were so apologetic that day that Maebh had wondered how many drunken husbands were returned to their wives for fixing in this country.

It's as thunder grey when Ailis, JC and Maebh head down to the beach again as it has been every cloudy night after 4 p.m. You can hardly see anything but the white crests of the waves which are pulling Maebh into them except she doesn't want to die in that cold, not while there's more pie and a film to catch back at the house. Maebh lets Ailis's little hand steer her straight.

"Why are we here JC?" she asks. "It's like the setting of an especially bleak off-season Neil Jordan film." He stares straight ahead holding Ailis's other hand. You can't hear a thing in this din.

The crowds will start coming soon to the beach with the warm weather after they leave but avoiding them is what Maebh wants. She fears the eyes that might pretend to know her before they should. Living abroad allows for greater anonymity. She felt it in Paris at first till familiarity wore it thin. Maybe no place is really hers and she's best flitting about from port to port—a tossed glassy metamorphic cliché—till she's worthy of getting to know.

They come upon the sheep down there marching off like grey clouds over the sand and will see them marching a week later along the highway.

It's time for them to get out of there too. The magic of the fog has dissipated and Maebh might need sun to get better. Gaofei had told her about a job teaching in Spain so she had taken it. More wandering could help till she realizes no amount of sunshine can fade whatever is chasing her on, and she might as well stay put.

—

Up in Belfast, at her Granny's birthday a week before Maebh and JC leave for Spain, Maebh sits with her cousin Grainne, who tells her about her last trip to the Canary Islands.

"But isn't it lovely and warm here for once!" she says. "All the roses are out in Granny's garden. By next year they'll have climbed all the way to the third story."

Maebh does love the gardens in Ireland. There are daffodils in February, rosemary all year long and many houses have climbing roses up them like Granny's.

Grainne's daughter, Dervla, is the same age as Ailis and they sit together in the large family photo with their daughters on their laps. They have alcoholic, politically-disillusioned fathers and are the first of the cousins to have children, and the only to do so before they are twenty six. Grainne's father is the Secretary of the Communist Party in Northern Ireland and he and Maebh's grandparents might be the only communists in Northern Ireland.

"The Ulster revisionist Army didn't take too well to communists so Granny and Granda had to leave their homes in the centre of town for the quiet suburban enclave on Strangford Lough," Grainne says.

Maebh listens, happy to learn some things about the family she sees once every year if she's lucky. Also, Ailis has a cousin to play

with till that cousin, Grainne's daughter, steals her cookie and everyone laughs.

"She's a chip off the old block!" her grandfather says.

Granny comes over after the photo to give them both five thousand pounds.

"You need this money more than anyone else in the family," she says, "and I've more than I need since Granda died so I don't see why you should wait for me to go as well."

Everyone else is pretty well off on Maebh's mother's side of the family and Grainne and Maebh are the poor ones, but Grainne owns a small house she can now refurbish.

"We can paint up the place with this and put in a modern kitchen," she says.

Maebh holds her cheque in her hands—it will more than cover their flights to Spain but she has no idea what to do with it beyond that. Five thousand pounds, she will later learn, is almost enough for a down payment to buy a house if she only knew how to plan a life out, but it will disappear stupidly in her hands as money does. She doesn't really understand finance beyond everyday rent and food. But now there is another problem.

JC who was singing the Russian national anthem with Maebh and Grainne's fathers is all of a sudden crawling on all fours through the living room, gasping for air, with a sausage roll spitting from his mouth. Everyone is alarmed and screaming, except Maebh who is helping Ailis find another cookie. However, he was choking to death, and might have died for the billionth time if Orla, her other cousin—the sharp-tongued doctor one, who would never need five thousand pounds from anyone—had not wrapped both arms just under his ribs and forced the mashed-up other half of the sausage roll from his mouth. JC flails about, knocking over a few things, holding his throat. Everyone offers him comfort, but Maebh doesn't even get up from her seat to help him.

—

"I love your little apricots," JC says to Maebh, a week before they leave for Spain. He comes up behind her to hold her breasts gently in his hands—something he has never done and she sees a look in his eyes she doesn't recognize from the mirror as he undresses her. She lets him take everything off and helps him with her jeans because he seems to be crying. And then he kisses her hair so softly Maebh is amazed, she could cry too but cannot. Romance for anything but the Irish greens outside has all but died in her. His sentiments are too late. She remembers reaching her arms and legs round him looking for love and the rotting smell in his mouth from his blackened teeth and somehow her body moves with his but without responding as it should. The memory of his previous lack of affection is too strong and all the times she begged for it.

"Maybe we can make a new start of it in Spain?" he says moving slowly, trying to look into her eyes, but Maebh is watching their long sickly forms—grey-white on pink-white—in the mirror, uninspired. The body that used to be her is silent with arm muscles like tennis balls sticking out of its frame. All the times she had carried Ailis under her coat to protect her from the rain that too often came down when they had hiked the forty-five minutes from the cliff house to the pub where the bus picked them up. Ailis always fit her arms and legs tight round Maebh, as tight as Maebh now tries to fit all her exhaustion into JC, wishing he could just carry her for a little bit.

She holds herself as close to JC as she can after he climaxes, relieved it comes quickly. Glad that she let him but wishing she knew how to climax too—wishing he had done this more and earlier and that she knew how to ask him to caress her and do other things as well—things she hadn't even figured out.

She lies listening to JC breathing. She isn't alone. Some intimacy from the man she can't love is better than none.

14

They •rive from Granny Sisi's on Strangfor• Lough near Belfast,
the high ti•e fills up to the long grasses by the walls
an• the low ti•e pulls out muck as far as the eye can see.

They hea• along the farm roa•s to Granny Joan's in Derry.
The motor in the car hums through the green and purple landscapes
too painful to •escribe. You wa•e through with your eyes as
they turn harder by the barb wire at the checkpoint.

An• then the light blue of Granny Joan's eyes.
They have too much in them like hers.

Granny Joan presses the small pink beads into Maebh's hands
seven an• one, seven an• one, five times, plus three an• then one again.
She prefers her apple pie with sprinkle• sugar an• homema•e ice cream.

Mary of the sorrows will save her an• her son—thorns, nu•ity—
the stories an• cruste• gol• roun• the myth of them.

At first communion, her uncle spoke softly
—smiley in his vestments—a wee •ram of whiskey.
She knows her dress is short, eyes wide to the arches,
hymns an• rockabye spaces—Go• on lips an• cheeks.

Sinea• an• Maebh run from home to the bus in Toronto
up the steps to the choristry, the organ pipes and the choir mistress with ringlets.

At confession, she asks why her parents •on't believe but meant really something else.

The priest has eyes elsewhere, touche• or in•ifferent—
"Three Hail Marys an• one Our Father!"

15

JC finds the bar in the old part of town. It's on a tiny corner, a faded blue exterior with thick splinters of bare wood showing through and similarly painted tables and benches that spill out onto the tight street. He goes there with Ailis most days and Maebh meets them after teaching. They eat grilled pulpo on sticks that feels like it should but doesn't stick to the teeth and a wine that is both strong and young, the way a new wine might with grapes baked in southern Spain. Ailis plays on the cobbled street. Maebh doesn't remember any cars but maybe there were a few. It's twisty and narrow but some vehicles are so tiny and the drivers of such skill they might easily manoeuvre through. When JC is not chatting, the sound of TV in the corner playing bullfights entertains. Maebh stares at the legs and puffed chests of the Matadors swirling in capes of decadent satin. And she plays at this with Ailis and her jacket—letting her rush through, back and forth like a little bull—"*Toro, toro*!"

This café is their haven in this would-be paradise Cartagena, a working class town in southern Spain with a military tanker parked at the beach. The wide avenues downtown are too well swept and ladies walk the marble sidewalks in ironed blouses with gold buttons, enjoying the shade from gleaming white high rises on either side. There are palm trees with bunches of flowers at their feet and street vendors selling egg and potato tortilla but basically Maebh and JC want to leave despite the dead weight of welcome sunshine that hits as soon as they arrive.

The job is terrible. She can't imagine what possessed her to teach young children at a school and in a city she knew nothing about. She was hired ostensibly because any mother should know how to teach young children but Maebh stands aimlessly in class wondering why they aren't snivelling in protest and she knows that if they did she could not stop them. She almost wishes they'd start an uproar for their own sakes or that they could escape out to the streets together for a romp through the park. But they seem to have had a sense of order instilled into them. Maebh sings songs and tries to teach them the words—head, shoulders, knees and toes. She draws a body of a child on the board and labels the different body parts. And then she repeats the damn song over and over again with the gestures. It's exhausting. They are learning the colours in Spanish so she gives them red crayons to scribble over a fire engine truck. They all colour delicately in the lines, even though Maebh doesn't think fire engines are red. Her failure here triggers her failure as a mother to get her own child talking and the realization that motherhood requires skills beyond love and effort to get right.

Whenever she tries to sit down to plan a lesson, the owner glares from her horn-rimmed glasses. There is no tolerance for lesson planning or time wasting and Maebh is sent down to help with the toddlers. They want her to change diapers but she doesn't. Their diapers smell like nothing she's ever had to deal with since she fed Ailis one of those store-bought jars and the stench of her stools was too much to bear. Ailis has since then only been given mashed up homemade foods and breast milk. And her diapers hardly smell. High food standards are one aspect of motherhood Maebh can muster—that, and clothing. She and Ailis both look well enough to be granted entrance through the front door almost with a look of pride from the owner before Maebh realizes she's to go in by the back and wear a dark green polyester uniform.

Maebh rides the school bus to and from the school. She's asked to stand up and watch the children but that makes her nauseous so she slouches at a window, browsing the streets, ignoring the resentful glances of the other teachers and resentful herself that the school seems to think they own every second of their persons. She sits at the back of the bus guarding her interior self from the job clock-in machine that calculates her productivity while the other teachers talk about her. The working population seems enslaved here which challenges running assumptions that southern countries lie about in the sunshine while northern Europeans have the work ethic to emulate. Northern Europe might outperform Southern Europe but it's not for lack of effort. The problem seems more complicated, or maybe even a convenient exaggeration.

After teaching Maebh wants to go to bed but the evenings are hard to miss. The streets shine with colours, food and people everywhere. The days are long in Spain and Maebh has no idea when or if anyone ever sleeps. At JC's old-world bar, she's conscious that it isn't really an establishment women frequent. She sits there extra delicate in a white linen shirt and black jeans with crossed legs and head down sipping wine. She's drinking just a drop some days, long enough to forget for a brief moment that she's still breastfeeding a bit at night and not yet her own person. The wine is cheap, red, and reconnects her to something essential that has escaped since the love and fatigue of motherhood. But with wine she contemplates things in a rhyming roundabout way in her mind, wondering as she always does if there is a way to reach for a pen without breaking the spell. She hasn't kept a notebook handy since the early days in Paris— maternity kills creativity, or is it the bad planning? JC has re-found himself midst the sloppy overflowing wine, too, and let go of the touching Irish sadness that was starting, or might have started, to endear him to Maebh.

The warmth has its effect too and Maebh can feel the infection in her chest loosening and a glow coming back to her skin. The air—the hub of everyday life at the bar, the proud matadors and the strangers wading in and out with little conversations and head nods of recognition place her in a kind of quiet and welcome a return to life. JC is right beside her and Ailis is on her lap, but she feels as if they are not there and that she has been given time to ponder what's percolating around her. Being truly alone can have a way of closing you up inside loneliness, which is not conducive to the kind of magic Maebh is now enjoying. Being alone with family round you is a secret protected loneliness you can enjoy without the awkward pity and interference of strangers.

The bullfighters on the TV screen parade into the arena with the poor bull. Maebh counts six of them. There are gaudy fellows on horseback and Maebh wonders why the party is so large, but then as is the case with any spectacle, she likes where it takes her more than what occurs in front of her. She is the bull—pricked and irritated as it's that time of the month and she's getting her period again. Or maybe, the bull and her, are ambivalent. She can't tell. She feels his bulk drawn into the game poised for action but also imagines he'd rather be lolling in a daisy field somewhere. Are they mocking him or serenading him—challenging death or bowing before it? The banderilleros stab the bull precisely but with flamboyance till the blood runs down his sides. Everyone in the arena leans in. The bull is fierce but only because they've irked him on. She can't watch too closely but is more intrigued than sickened, trying to understand the need for the whole challenge in the first place. She shuffles Ailis from one leg to another and then crosses her legs again—remembering that there are no other women here. She comes out of her thoughts and feels the outline of her femininity in the evening shadows of the bar in defiance. For these men who disapprove of her being there, she too is likely the bull—an ignorant, powerful innocent to be suspicious of and tamed.

JC slams his fist on the table all of a sudden.

"I need another drink!"

He's turned nasty again and leaps up and down until she gives him money. Now that she has money from her grandmother, controlling his alcoholism is impossible, especially in a country where it's more accessible than bottled water.

"I'm out of cash!" she says.

"Well let's get some from the machine," he says and he stands up and starts jumping up and down, glaring violently and without caring how he looks.

She is about to oblige. She's the bull with the money who doesn't stand a chance.

The owner of the restaurant seems to understand and though he doesn't look at her or like her being there, she senses he appreciates her dilemma and because he's gracious and proud to have foreigners in his bar he comes over with a glass for JC.

"*Gratos*!" he says to JC, who is beaming because he likes nothing more than being offered a drink though he never returns the favour.

The owner talks to JC in bursts of Spanish and English about the dynamics of this particular bullfight. JC compliments his bar and the people of Cartagena and the bullfight of course. They converse with passionate gestures and seem to understand each other. The bull is *la mujer*, JC says. And then another gentleman, Kallu from Finland nods in agreement from the table beside them.

"A female with long hair pulled back like in *Guernica*."

"Ah yes!" says JC, "Picasso loved the bullfight. Americans die hugging bears in Yellowstone park like it's Disneyland but not the Spanish. They know the matador is in a precarious dance he only survives with much guile."

"That's how a man survives with a female," Kallu says.

"*Exactamente*!" says the barman who seems to understand English whenever it suits him.

"Congratulations on your beautiful family," Kallu says, raising his glass to Ailis and Maebh. "When you have females like that, being a matador is a privilege."

"But what if I'm the Matador fighting you animals around me?" says Maebh, having decided somewhere between the wine, interior ramblings and the garish embroidery of the bullfight costumes, that this scenario is as possible as the other and that all these male-female divisions are nonsense when we all must fight to survive.

"No, that's not possible! " says JC. "You have given birth, are the giver of life—what part has a man in that?"

"Very little!" Maebh says, "if you watch on with as little sympathy as you did."

"What need has a woman to battle the bull, when she is intrinsically connected with nature herself?" Asks Kallu. "Man has only this way to face it."

"You suggest then that a woman has no issue to battle with nature just because she gives birth or that she should ask a man to battle for her?" she asks.

She has had this conversation before, with Maxim even. Woman is this and that. Woman is something men know better than women when men pretend she is a mystery.

"That is what art is about!" JC says in exasperation, "fighting against the demands of nature and woman."

"But what is a man if he is not fighting to win the heart of woman," says Kallu trying to bring chivalry back to the table. He raises his glass again and Maebh likes the way he looks at her but this conversation makes her sad.

"Women have the same fights," she says, or begs with a shaky voice, hoping he will understand. She looks at Kallu when she says this because his interpretation is preferable, willing him to get it. But wanting the argument to end all the same, wondering what is it about 'woman' and that damn apple and what Simone de Beauvoir calls her otherness, that denies her humanity. Her neutrality has been stripped of her and she has not been allowed to be a priest or a Jesus figure or any being facing what it means to be alive beyond sex and maternity and a creature too old, too young or just right for fucking, and fucking at this point in Maebh's life feels sickening except maybe not with Kallu.

Maebh is heated up now with her thoughts, and blushing slightly, and the bull is running frantic with sticks jabbed into his neck.

"Brava!" says JC applauding loudly.

"Why don't they just kill it with one clean cut?" she says. 'Wouldn't that demand greater skill and humanity?"

"This is the second stage in the bullfight," Kallu says. "The bull is already weak and hopefully the matador has learned how he moves and which side he likes to attack from. The banderilleros have stabbed the bull and now he is angry and attacks more ferociously."

"But why must he suffer so much?" she says.

"*Tu comprenٛs rien!*" says JC. "It's not like animals are slaughtered with any dignity by you clean freak Americans. We are all here to suffer!"

"Sure, and I can see the art of bringing some majesty to that but..." she says.

"It's a dance involving man's often unsavoury relationship with nature," Kallu says. His grey eyes follow her face. "And the matador doesn't always win. He needs to show that both he and the bull are worthy foe, worthy of a proper death and strong enough to take it."

Maebh listens, intrigued.

"Have you read Lorca's poem 'A los cinco de la Tarde'?"

"No!" she says.

"I'll get you a copy," he says.

"I've seen Almodovar's film, though, and it has a female matador."

"You aren't letting go of that."

"The matador is back in the ring," says JC.

"He has fifteen minutes to kill the bull," says Kallu.

"I'm not sure I want to see this," Maebh says.

She remembers again that she has her period and needs to make sure she's not about to bleed all over the place herself. Thank god she's wearing black jeans. The barman leads her to the toilet and inspects them first to make sure they are clean. Ailis wants to come with her but Maebh manages to convince her to stay with JC, who tells her a story about bull calves with flowers in their hair and the great god Pan serenading them with his flute. Maebh is not bleeding anymore, thank goodness, but she changes her tampon anyway. There's still hardly any weight on her. She wraps the barely-sullied tampon in a bit of toilet paper and puts it in the bin beside the sink. It's just a bit of blood from an egg that never found its mate and nothing about the flushing of it out of her body is that extraordinary, Maebh thinks, still riled up and angry even. Nor has her period made her feel creative in any way or closer to understanding the mysteries of life which mystify her as much as they must mystify men. On good days like today, she can just ignore her period until an accident happens and it's leaking everywhere.

"The poor old suffering bull," she says to Ailis as she comes back to the table. "Let him die easily!" Maebh has never feared death as much as suffering—life being so much crueler.

"The first Matadors were women by the way," Kallu says smiling, as she puts Ailis back on her lap. "Women in Crete danced with bulls four thousand years ago and Goya painted the legendary female bullfighter Nicolasa Escamilla in the 1770's."

"So what was once a fertility rite has turned into a test of macho virility?" she asks.

"Sort of!" says Kallu. "It might be a shift from a homage to nature to a homage to civilization."

"*Toro*!" says Ailis, cuddling up happily into her mother's arms, eyes glued to the TV.

"Hopefully, my little bullfighter," Maebh whispers round Ailis's curly head, "you will never have to deal with this shit." Except what Kallu says is interesting and the colours in the arena are majestic and Maebh almost tears up at the spectacular demonstration of courage, skill and heightened emotion and feels motivated as she steps out into the drab little street and her drab little life to move forward differently.

That night they invite Kallu back to their apartment for dinner. JC quickly does a tomato salad while Maebh puts Ailis, who is already asleep, into bed. JC cuts up some *jamón* and bread with it and a strange-smelling cheese. Kallu doesn't seem to have much money either and his thin frame leans over the food eagerly. Maebh fusses over the table a bit more than normal, arranging the plates and glasses. Kallu could tone down the smarm but she enjoys feeling his light eyes on her body and watching him eat like he hasn't all day.

"A beautiful woman and beautiful food—lucky you, JC," Kallu says.

"Beauty!" Maebh says to him sitting down, "what does that even mean?"

"I'm not sure but someone once said it's in the eye of the beholder," Kallu says smiling. "Actually, I do most of the cooking and shopping," says JC, his mouth full of food, and he pours himself more wine like their glasses aren't even there.

"How long have you been here?" Maebh asks. He is beautiful and she likes looking at him as much as he seems to like looking at her.

"About six months."

"But why would you stay that long?" says JC. "We thought of leaving as soon as we got here."

"I've even applied for another teaching job in Murcia," Maebh says. "It's a much cooler town."

"I like it here in the middle of nowhere," he said. "I'm fed up with good taste."

"But there's not even an anti-vibe here my friend," says JC.

"Exactly," Kallu says.

Maebh watches Kallu in his grey linen suit from another time, and way too thick for the weather, even if he has his shirt unbuttoned low over his thin chest. She notices, also, that he hasn't finished his first glass of wine in the time JC almost downed the rest of the bottle. He made the place more durable but still he needs fixing and seems no better at feeding himself than JC. Maebh can't explain why he attracts her so.

That night after Kallu leaves, Maebh presses herself close to JC in bed and squirms out of her nightie. She places JC's hands on her hip and moves it gently up and down for him from her breasts to her bum till he starts doing it himself startled by the effect it has on her. Maebh imagines Kallu watching them. It's the closest she ever comes to having an orgasm with JC. Her disinterest in intimacy might be coming to an end and she might even be imagining another life for herself. Strange though that she can love JC better when she doesn't any longer.

—

Maebh gets fired from the kindergarten the day after they go to the beach at La Mancha. A thin peninsula paradise ruined by a British and German tourist highway, lined with high-rises on either side, all the way up. They almost have the beach to themselves, and while the sun comes and goes, and the water could be warmer, they do swim. Still the white wall of empty high-rises at their backs cements their hatred of this place, so Maebh's almost glad when she receives the termination letter.

She had been standing in class, all week, with no idea even how to wing it with these kids, her confidence abandoned under their feet. She gave them green crayons for frog and grass and tree and thought about walking out the front door, except movement of any kind didn't seem worth it.

The owners of the school inform the landlord of their new situation and they find that they have till the end of the week to vacate the place. She gets an interview with the language school in Murcia and for a moment a more exciting life in Spain teaching adults presents itself.

"We don't need anyone right away," the owner tells her, "but you never know when we will."

She has enough money to move into a cheaper place in Spain and hang out for a bit but Maebh is all of a sudden so tired she can feel a curtain about to shut her mind. Two jobs lost in two years, a husband she doesn't love, a small child to feed and an empty notebook filled with aspirations.

Packing up is difficult as Maebh had felt compelled once again to bring everything with them. They have bags of clothes for all seasons, toys for Ailis, books and homey knick-knacks in three large suitcases. She has also turned inexplicably into a clean freak and scrubs the brand new stove they hardly used like she has never cleaned anything in her life.

"You don't have to!" the landlord's daughter assures her while the landlord looks on like she can't wait to have them out of there. But it's one of those bright modern apartments a scrap of grease turns tragic and Maebh needs to leave things pristine behind her because whatever she's stepping into is so precarious and because everything she touches turns to crud.

She's heading back to Ireland with Ailis and JC is going to Paris. She'll stay with her parents till she figures out what to do and imagines JC will find someone to stay with. He always does and she has no desire to worry about him anymore. She has dragged him over Europe hoping to find a way but there doesn't seem to be one. Her parents will take her in but wouldn't have JC back. He drank through their whole liquor cabinet the last time and smashed his fists through the dining room glass doors when they locked the booze up there.

She gives him the chunk of money from her grandmother, or she lets him bully it off her. He jumped up and down in a tantrum till she did, and she finally tells him she will give it to him if he takes them to the airport, which he wasn't planning on doing.

"What a nightmare my life is with you!" he says pocketing the cash. "It's the least you can do."

She can't imagine how she and Ailis are going to get through the airport with all their life possessions without him, but a taxi and a porter would have been cheaper than the three thousand odd pounds she hands him. This unfortunately doesn't occur to her, nor that she should never have given him any money at all. She is too dumb or pathetic to keep just a little of it for herself. She does know that she will manage and seems to believe too much in her own infallibility. Perhaps this is what she needs to reconcile.

JC will stop to visit friends in Barcelona before heading back to Paris, while Ailis and Maebh get stuck in Heathrow for ten hours without a penny for the extra baggage fees they get charged on their connecting flight. Her parents will wire over funds.

Ailis and she wait in the lounge with all those suitcases—the ones she almost wanted to just leave there. One of the security guards gives them food tickets for a meal. But the other personnel refuse to believe her story. They seemed ready to before they saw her. Even this low, she looks too posh and chipper to be in a condition she can't articulate—that is, penniless, husbandless, jobless and despised. But she is not rock bottom and has more to lose yet. The bright lights and bland sofas at the airport make this hard to grasp. Ailis and she shuffle from seat to seat, to entertain themselves, row after row after row, pushing the trolley along with them. Then she plays the *toro* game with her. Ailis runs headlong into the coat with elbows pointed outwards for horns. But Maebh is holding the coat out with too limp a sweep. Ailis looks up with some criticism as if she knows her mother is stuck in Heathrow airport in a chasm of her own ineptitude.

16

They go back to Toronto after •a• comes
but first Roisin is born in Lisburn.

Mum says Roisin will be able to see colours at six weeks
and Maebh wakes early on this date
with an array of bright objects to show her.

Mum and Dad do their thing, Sinead excels at gymnastics
so Roisin is her secret crush.

"What's your name?" the UVF guy ha• aske• Da•
"Murray!"
"Which Murrays?"

It's usually a Protestant name but the guy seemed
to already know Dad was Catholic and they went back to Toronto.

When Roisin is sixteen months, they have a brother—James.
They live in Da•'s office on Berkeley St. till they can buy another house.
It's on a row of grey stuccos with little cobble• si•ewalks an• birch trees outside
cool business stuff all roun• an• the lake is there big as a sea but you can't get to it.

"The •amn city trappe• the water behin• the freeway!" Da• says

James scrunches up in your arms so easy to carry
an• Roisin walks at nine months
she crawls into the toilet bowls and through waves at the beach

But Mum and Dad have two babies in their bedroom
an• Sinea• an• Maebh have been forgotten.

Alone, they take their bath and curl up in towels with the hair dryer to warm them,
Maebh win•s the alarm clock before be• an• in the morning they make breakfast,
pack a lunch with whatever the fin• in the fri•ge an• •ig for bus fare in the couch cushions
that fall out wherever Da• sat an• they always arrive late for school.

On the weekend, they take the laundry on their backs
in garbage bags like giant beetles to Queen and Parliament.
They take all of •a•'s socks an• all the towels.
Nobody even asked them too.

It was better than wearing
•irty clothes pulle• from the wash basket.
They buy Frito-Lays from the bills Da• gives them to make change
an• then mini boxes of Ti•e with re• Frito-fingers, stan•ing on tippy-toe,
from the •ispensers on the wall.

They go home and back again
to drag the pants and shirts and pillow-cases
all twiste• out from the trolleys into the mammoth •ryers
that could have eaten them but didn't.

Mum feels guilty an• gives them allowance but Da• says fuck'em
with the strong cheese and black rye bread, hard and crumbly, he prefers.
Da• has one part-time job, two full-time jobs an• for solace too many nights at the bar.

Sinea• grows tire• of this an• leaves Maebh to wash an• •ry the •ishes
and make the porkchops on her own in the evenings.

She starts to wet the bed at night and begs Maebh
to walk with her to the toilet but it's just next door.

On good days they pile into the snow piles
with socks and mittens high over their trousers and sweaters under their snowsuits.
Maebh wraps scarves roun• their faces to keep off the win•.

Then Sinead drank her holy water and stole her savings
to buy Fruit Loops cause she just wanted to try them once.

Such a banal list of gru•ges to har•en a heart

"Maebh, please, there are ghosts in the corri•or!"

Sinea• even saw one with a knife when the guy across the street was murdered.

Maebh is not sure why Sinea• never calle• her parents—
like Maebh, she has forgotten they are there.

"Please, please!" Sinea• begge•.

Maebh lies still in the third bunk.
If she gave in to nee•, it woul• tear her asun•er.

These are her sins.

17

Maebh spends a few months staring at a wall in the house her parents rent in Rathgar. The cat they found as a runt sleeps on her bed and fleas bite her legs. The black that has shut down her mind thinks they at least should find some use for her. There is no trace of whatever had set her off through Europe or any of the resulting emotions. A battery pack of feeling that is her heart is sitting somewhere and she has no interest in recharging it. At night, she spits up into tissues she leaves all over the house. She keeps her parents awake sometimes with her coughing and once her mum brings in some cognac to loosen up the phlegm and hopefully shut her up.

Ailis watches *Teletubbies*—glowing in raptures with coloured markers she already knows how to set off beautifully on paper while Maebh sits beside her, too useless for anything but putting the lids back on. The house feels empty without her siblings. Roisín is still at the Sorbonne, Sinead is in Toronto working as a production secretary for the film *To Die For* and James is sixteen but has gone back to stay with her because he stole too much from mum's wallet and got kicked out.

Maebh eats everything in the fridge or that's what her mum tells her aunts. Ailis sits on her lap at the table and twists a piece of skin on her neck. She leaves red marks with her fingernails to wake her mother up.

"I want boobie!" she says finally talking a bit.

She doesn't seem to amuse in the typical toddler way and this disappoints her grandparents who leave her in front of the telly as much as Maebh when they mind her. Apparently, two-and-a-half-year-olds act out plays and ask questions about the world, but Ailis, like Maebh, is moving in a deep love affair with silence. Maebh carries Ailis everywhere and doesn't know how to furnish the kind of instruction she requires. There's obvious intelligence in the child's eyes, loneliness in her face and fortunately joy, too.

The spare bedroom is being renovated when Maebh comes back. Mum had scraped off the wallpaper but doesn't paint it so there are still bits of glue and mouldy patches speckled over the plaster. Cracked lines run about from splotch to splotch and it looks ruined like an antique map as long as Maebh stays there. It'll do, like she has been abandoned to an asylum.

The whole house is a lovely Victorian—bigger than you'd think with stairs up and down in odd places but a bit damp and in need of repair. It's also next door to the house where James Joyce was born in a fairly affluent part of Dublin. There's a large walled-in square out front for members only that Ailis and Maebh walk round scorned by family types, as Maebh is too young and hip a mum to not be a cost to the state. There are so many young mothers abandoned like Maebh in a country where abortion is illegal and daycare more than rent so going to work is cruelly illogical.

The fleabag cat they call JJ for James Joyce spends most of his time in the room with them.

"All the best names start with J," JC had said when he had found the runt last summer in the garden.

He had fed him full fat cream from his fingertips and wee bits of kidney because that is what Leopold Bloom ate for breakfast. The tiny thing crawled about his shoulders and Maebh was amazed at how tender he was with animals. Now, he's in France visiting various friends and Maebh won't hear much from him till he's burnt through all the money she shouldn't have given him. Maebh is feeling better the morning he stops bragging about his exploits and sends his first I so miss you letter. She sees it at the front door, picks it up and puts it away for later.

Dad is there tapping away at the articles he's writing on AIDS and blood trade corruption in Ireland. Drafts and research are stacked up high on the table till they get moved to the piano for dinner.

"There are some fried tomatoes leftover in the pan and a bit of bacon," Dad says looking up from his computer and trying to make a little room for them at the table.

"Thanks!" Maebh says putting Ailis down in the chair beside him with her toy animals.

"And there are loads of eggs to fry up."

Mum isn't here so she doesn't mind opening the fridge. She turns the gas on and pushes the tomatoes over in dad's copper pan to make room for two eggs. She's feeling hungry for the first time in weeks and her face looked like something when she put her cream on and she might even walk into town with Ailis.

"Here!" Dad says ripping an article from his computer. "It's a review of the *Northrop Frye on Shakespeare* book I gave you last Christmas."

She had studied with Frye twice at the University of Toronto—second-year Shakespeare and then his Bible and mythology course. She had skimmed through the book which seemed to be an almost verbatim copy of his lectures, or at least the ones she hadn't missed before she realized attending them could be as inspiring as meandering through the college's neoclassical arches and shady courtyards.

"He's not a revolutionary like Marshall McLuhan," says Dad, who had studied with McLuhan when they first arrived in Canada in 1968.

"Frye's more entertaining than you might think, though," Maebh says. "Some people say he's just a codifier but what's the harm in that when you wrap up things so handily." And then she unveils this sentence as she walks back into the kitchen almost as if she's talking to herself. "Shakespeare is a movement, through marriage or mass slaughter, from dark to light, chaos to order, confusion to understanding and the Bible is fear of nature versus the hero who must be sacrificed in the name of universal salvation."

She seems to have summed up two years of lectures rather handily herself but it's stiff for over breakfast conversation, and Dad just nods absently.

He's more a McLuhan guy. "This newspaper and that screen define us culturally," he says, outlining a TV with his finger in mid-air because they have not always owned one. "McLuhan converted to Catholicism as an adult," he continues, "and I once had a conversation with him and Seamus Heaney about the United Empire Loyalist roots of waspy Canadian conservatism." He shuffles his papers with pride and looks his soft blue eyes up at her in amusement—"that bloody Heaney put his hand on my shoulder and said, 'Calm down now Murray,'" and that had Maebh laughing because he said it with the Northern Ireland accent which was faint to invisible these days.

"I'm not sure that Heaney is a match for Yeats, though," and then he goes on about the Troubles, occultism, Irish post-1960's wheelbarrow-by-the-bog poetry and how AIDS was concocted in a lab by the CIA to kill off black people in Africa.

"What ever happened to the blood book you sent to New York," she asks.

"I never heard back from them, but then they published a modified version of it under the name of a famous journalist," he said.

"Jeez!"

"I thought about suing them but the book never did very well."

"I'm sorry!"

"I used the research to uncover the same blood trade corruption here in Ireland for the paper and am up for an award, so it'll do," he says shrugging.

"Too bad Canada wouldn't publish it," Maebh says.

"They just don't have money for chances."

Maebh looks at her dad with respect. She and Roisín had assumed that he just hadn't gotten it together to finish it. She cuts up the bacon for Ailis, wipes the bit of egg off her chin and puts the baby spoon in her hand.

"They didn't want to get sued either," he adds.

His writing has always taken over the house—he can write on any subject but is best when given an assignment. That book was the first time he had written something of his own, so Maebh feels bad for him that it didn't do better.

"You might find me lying face down in my own vomit one day like it's an accident. That's how 'they' do in guys like me."

He has been talking about 'they' for years, whoever 'they' is, and Maebh wants to say she believes things more random, that no one is in charge, that a hundred years ago the creepy watching 'they' would have been god. But she doesn't, and who knows, he could be right.

She watches him typing quickly now with two fingers. He can jump back into his article in fits and starts, in and out of conversation at random. He won't work in an office and seems to have that ability to thrive off family noise. Maebh supposes if he were her age he'd write best in an after-hours joint. She's irked he gets to sit around, apart from his much lauded gastronomic forays in the kitchen, contemplating the universe while mum pushes the vacuum about his legs with that look on her face; but she is proud people round town talk about his column.

He looks up again and passes her a big brown file envelope with some tickets and information on a modern dance group.

"It's a press pack," he says.

"Oh!"

"I thought you could write a review," he says.

Maebh had studied ballet till she was eighteen and had written a few articles for the university papers but had never imagined he thought her capable of doing anything more. He did get her to read his book, so maybe he thinks more highly of her than he lets on.

Maebh fingers through the contents of the envelope—primordial shapes and drumming with bones. A dark shape of her own shifts on by. Her first reaction is blasé but then she's surprised to find this gesture has brought life into her. She had liked being turned off. It was like having all pain and feeling removed from her person and she is not sure she is ready yet to feel that again, but her body has decided otherwise.

"Thanks!" she says and there's music in her voice. She's blushing with gratitude and a sense that perhaps her parents do care about her. She wonders if it took getting so low to provoke a reaction.

Dad is looking at her intently and seems to have noticed she's perked up but he gets up quickly.

"Coffee?" he asks.

"Maybe," she says. Sometimes she drinks it to keep him company because she enjoys these talks.

"You're too much like your mum," he says, which is of course nothing any young woman hoping for more than a second-fiddle life behind her husband wants to hear. She's quite the lightweight when it comes to alcohol too, glad he's given that up since he came to Ireland. He will pick it up again with a vengeance in a few years though.

"I'm not an alcoholic and can stop anytime," he will say. "But sobriety is for assholes!"

At least, he has never smoked. Maebh likes the idea of these addictions—who wants to be a prude?—but then you feel so crappy after and she prefers an apple anyway.

"Free love is over," Dad says coming back with two full cups as she gingerly pastes a bit of egg, tomato and bacon on her fork. Her taste buds are still numbed but at least she now wants to taste.

"AIDS put an end to the best part of the 70's and 80's," Dad says explaining the gory details of how it spreads. "And they tried to blame sex and gay men!"

"Maybe now men will worry about condoms as much as women," is all Maebh can say as she tries to get a few extra bits of egg into Ailis.

Dad looks at her angrily. "Men have had it worse, Maebh, conscripted to mass slaughters on the battlefields, sodomy in the priesthood, and a long life providing for a household of brats and their mother," he says.

It's not like he comes out with the declaration but she knows he thinks all a woman need do is find a good man, love her children and remain attractive doing so. She's relieved his fear for her mental health has overpowered his conviction that she shouldn't need anything important to do beyond this. She fingers through the contents of the press pack, amazed again at the effect it has had on her and that she almost feels again like the girl at university before she ruined her life.

Then without thinking and in all of two minutes, she puts the breakfast dishes in the dishwasher including Dad's, which are in the sink, wipes down the counter and washes and dries the copper pot. She bundles up Ailis's animals, the brown envelope and Northrope Frye piece, makes a quick sweep to make sure nothing else betraying her existence haunts the room, and heads upstairs with Ailis to get ready for a walk.

These men/women talks run counter to undefined instincts she has to the contrary. As a child, her father had carefully explained to her, when she complained that their brother never did dishes, that men just weren't built with hands for kitchens and diapers. She had looked down at her own ten-year-old hands already so adept at household chores hating them, and how much she had willingly helped out mum from her earliest memories without being asked, and how this was somehow proof that she was destined for that kind of life.

At the time, she had tried to explain that it was a lot for mum managing four kids and that financial stresses were a lot for him and that it would be nice for them to share a bit but it seemed he had no time for this.

"We just have different talents," he had said. "It's wired in our brains."

"But you spend hours in the kitchen," she had said, knowing the art of cooking, the way he does it, is a divine act of inspiration and something a lot more women would be up for if they weren't bogged down with thankless chores.

"Sure women can make money and contribute intellectually," he had finally relented. And she had seen so clearly how women had been trapped into tidiness by some unfounded idea that they were the gentler sex and that that is why so many girls proudly proclaimed their bitchiness these days. She had had no interest in bitchiness and had never hated dishes so a riot raged within her person about where to place herself.

"Women just don't have it!" he had said mumbling about with his papers. "It" being, she supposed, that ability a man has to tune out the thankless stuff that might keep him from whatever project he wants to work on. "But they do have beauty and love," and he had looked at her gently as if what he was saying would sort her out. And she did wish she had wanted what he said she should want.

Maebh is glad she is already dressed in yesterday's outfit because otherwise she would have no idea what to wear. She welcomes the swell of Handel's *Messiah* blasting through the floorboards and Dad's beautiful baritone along with it—"And he shall reign forever and ever!" Maebh hates Handel but can't resist the urge to dance. She sweeps her arms over her head with windmill ballet arch. You might still be able to tell she was almost, but could never have been, good enough. Not that she hadn't given it everything.

"Talent trumps all in the end!" Dad would say, but the Scarlatti character in the Miloš Forman *Amadeus* film was more bitter than she about that, and less doubtful.

Mum comes home now with some groceries and sings with him.

"King of Kings, forever and ever."

She and Dad have their shtick and seem to have figured out things better than Maebh. There are only four years between them, but Mum remains the wide-eyed seventeen-year-old in bloomers when she fell pregnant with Maebh and he, though only a student at Queen's University Belfast editing the school paper, the wise man of words. Today, Mum can barely punctuate a sentence while dad quotes readily from Keats and Coleridge. Still, they enjoy great passion. You can see that from Mum's poses in the photos. Dad never poses though, and that's another frustrating question, or distinction perhaps, between the genders. Maebh likes to see herself in both of them but has trouble working through it. Some sense of defiance and conformity creates an impasse between whatever if anything it means to be male or female and why she needs to be anything at all.

Dad's tweed coat has been hanging from the same hook in the front hall since she got here, so she puts it on. It's a soft grey day but there's a chill in the air. Dad is looking gentle at the table and Mum is pushing all his papers into a pile with feigned irritation.

"Hallelujah, Hallelujah, Hal-le-lujah."

Maebh wishes she could sing along with them but the words are trapped down her throat and she has never felt part of their love. Mum is heavier than usual and looks only a few years older than Maebh. Dad's only fifty or so but has hair almost white, combed back with a slight wave old-school style. Still in well-cut navy trousers, pale pink shirt and Italian tan oxfords, he's too hip to be old, which confuses, as it contradicts with, the firm, even traditional, ideas he has about a few things. Maebh unfolds the stroller, relieved, as she always is, that there are no steps out the door. She puts Ailis in her coat and hat, wraps a thick blanket round her to keep the weather off her, and hooks her bag over the handles.

"I'm cooking lamb chops for lunch," Dad says as she runs back to the kitchen to get some biscuits and an apple for Ailis. He is dousing the pan with cumin, mint and red peppercorn. Sometimes he mashes the spices up himself with a mortar and pestle.

'How to judge a man but by who he is beside himself any given Tuesday?' she thinks.

"Thanks Dad!" she says stuffing the snacks into her bag.

"Oh Cal—you've spilt cumin all over the floor and your new shoes," Mum says laughing.

"Bye Mum," Maebh says.

She closes the door to the warmth in the house with some difficulty and moves herself off in the cool air with quick feet one in front of each other.

"Mummy's feeling better, Ailis, and we are going to the dole office for some money," she says tucking a stray bit of blanket round her and passing her a spongy giraffe.

The guy at the office asks her where she's been and if she's been out of the country. She tells them she was with her parents and too depressed to leave the house. She was depressed—the worst she's ever been but the rest is a cover-up because she can't explain why she couldn't change twenty diapers at a time in Spain, or how she gave all of Granny's early inheritance money to her alcoholic husband.

She puts the money he hands her in her wallet and heads over to a Montessori school at Merrion Square her cousin told her about for Ailis. She walks fast and then faster—it's easier with the pushchair and she passes people with almost reckless speed. The journalism gig has given her energy and a feeling she might actually not have completely ruined her life and if Ailis is having fun a few days a week maybe she can recover herself somewhat. And then she sees the sign for the language school on one of the smaller streets before the square—the Hushion School of English. She'll look their number up and give them a call at home.

"Hmn!" she says to Ailis, "Mummy is going to start teaching again."

There are a few nursery schools in front of the square Maebh notices so she decides to check them all out. Ailis needs someone happier than her miserable mother to play with. She's taken to TV cartoons and draws yellow splashes of sun and round little coloured figures but a flesh and blood creature to communicate with would be nice. Maebh is determined to choose an appropriate school for her. She didn't like the ramshackle one near her parents' with the overgrown yard and kids with dirty faces. She doesn't like the first one she comes to here either. The kids wear navy uniforms and take walks all tied up to a long rope but they don't like her either and redirect her to a school with a woman who looks like Maebh might in a few decades if she ever liked children as much. They take to each other right away and Ailis too and though it costs almost as much as her dole money to get her in there, Maebh signs her up starting tomorrow. They will walk forty-five minutes there rain or shine as Maebh can't fathom getting the pushchair on and off two packed buses during rush hour.

And Ailis will love her school, all the singing and games Maebh has never given her. "Ring around the rosie a pocket full of posies!" Her own parents certainly read and sang much more to Maebh and her siblings. Tomorrow, she will look back after Ailis's delighted little figure when she drops her off and feel the greatest relief that for once she is not failing her.

After securing a spot for Ailis and some literature about their program, Maebh turns the stroller home up to Grafton Street. Ailis wants to push the pushchair herself and the street is quiet so she unlocks the wheels and lets her walk with it swaying easily in all angles. They buy a sandwich to split at Bewley's for lunch and walk to Stephen's Green to see the ducks and swans and after they have eaten and chased the birds about a bit, Maebh puts Ailis back in the stroller and they head home through Rathmines Village. Maebh feels the last bit of money in her pocket and goes into a charity clothing shop because she sees a darling pale pink wool coat with a slightly darker musty rose hat for Ailis in the window. She also finds a pair of tan lace-up shoes with a small block granny heel for herself.

"What a score!" she says. "I can't believe the shoes are only just a pinch small. They look perfect with my grey tights and mini dress and the coat and hat are adorable on you Ailis with your red rubber boots."

She buys Mum a bouquet of freesia knowing that she should buy groceries instead but she doesn't quite know where to buy them and Mum just came home with two bags full earlier on. Or Maebh's just not feeling sufficiently herself yet to take on that much responsibility—some inertia or need to be irresponsible or balance the odds a bit makes her incapable.

Ailis is sleeping now so Maebh stops at a bookshop café. She finishes off her shopping therapy session with a used copy of *The Count of Monte Cristo.* It's amazing how having money cheers. She reminds herself to call the language school she just found for some work and starts in on the Dumas right then and there. There will be something about the hero's innocence and how patiently he rescues himself from ignorance and a prison fortress that inspires Maebh to uncover the smaller spiralling figurine of herself within herself.

She's not sure she is so innocent though. She has made too many purchases and wandered through Dublin like it was an empty beach. She needs to examine her behaviour as a chance to uncode the problems within it and why ever it is that she has been so artfully crossing and uncrossing her legs in the café willing the shopkeeper to look at them. So awkwardness and self-loathing return and settle in for the early evening when Ailis wakes and they walk back home.

The rain comes down but Ailis, who nibbles biscuits and apple under her rain hat, wrapped up tight in a blanket, never complains, and will grow up loving it as much as her mother. She'll even throw off the blanket and run home the last few blocks.

—

Maebh enjoys writing the dance review. She wonders while watching it why dance hasn't moved beyond the primitivism of Stravinsky's *Rite of Spring* in nearly a century and why it explores this without the same intensity, but she doesn't know how to fit that into her article—not being enough of an expert in the subject to do so. There could be a perfectly good reason or she's simply not confident enough in her instincts, but how could she be when no one ever knows enough. And all of a sudden she misses JC, now that her brain is not frozen and his letters have turned enquiring. He might have something to say on Stravinsky. They could walk together to the bar in the afternoons with wine or beer. Months of emptiness have gone by and feeling herself again has brought an urge to move into action but also a dimming of the past.

The review is adequate and her father publishes it. She uses her married name Danjou so it's easier and she doesn't look like his daughter. Her article is in *The Sunday Business Post* but she's not clued in enough to realize what a big deal it is and doesn't even keep a clip of it. After Christmas she starts researching a piece on French artisanal bread when she visits JC and his parents in the Sud-Ouest. His parents take her to speak to a baker in Albi about fermentation. Then, in Paris for a few days to visit Roisín, she interviews Lionel Poilane, a baker so acclaimed, he exports clumps of frozen fermented dough all the way to New York where they bake it fresh. Simply calling to get an interview on behalf of the newspaper had her ushered into his office a few days later with Earl Grey tea and a buttery apple tart. Poilane, who looks every inch the gentleman in charcoal tailored, double-breasted baker's jacket, tells her about how his father started making sourdough in 1932 and the origins of grey flour. He also compliments her person with genuine admiration.

Inspiration and beauty run high through her cheeks, she's so happy within the elegant combination of classical and modernist traditions in his office—the dark taupe walls, glass doors with wrought-iron frames, chandelier, antique desk and Vivaldi's "Winter" playing softly in the background.

Dad publishes this piece too. Maebh pushes regrets away and is a journalist. She starts socializing with Roisín's Trinity College friends when she comes back to Dublin, and, in the freshness of their youth, often forgets she's nearly a decade older than they, and a mother, and how she feels as if she has already died and gone to purgatory.

Dublin is a town where having the right accent and having read the right books separates you more than other places and Dubliners regularly tell her what a gas Dad's latest column was, so Maebh finds the upper ends of society more than she ever did in Toronto or Paris. These circles smell privilege off you, with a kind of cultured elitism she finds ugly but appreciates as it is to her benefit.

At some trendy do she goes to with Roisin, an economist says he has a story for her. He has written a book about Irish band hoarding in the music industry and wants her to help him bring it out. The record companies, he says, are signing up new bands, not to promote them but to eat up the competition which might destroy the mystique of U2 and the Cranberries. She gets interviews again saying she's with Dad's paper. She speaks to an indie music producer, the indie band Revelino and the head at EMI who explains that they promote as many bands as possible but that the bands most usually combust of themselves from pressure, in-fighting or lack of inspiration.

"Writing one good song is nowhere near as hard as writing ten for an album," he says, "and few manage."

Maebh details both points of view framed in how the story unravelled before her.

It's her best piece so far but the first paragraph comes out of nowhere so dad tells her to trash the whole thing without reading any further.

"I'm not going to publish any more of your articles," he says.

There's a strange look in his eyes, like now that's she's herself she'd better back off his turf. It's poor form to follow in his footsteps and not knock a path through on her own.

"You never even wanted to be a journalist," he says and because she can feel him willing her to give it up she doesn't say "but I'm good at it."

"Nepotism is not something I have ever admired," he continues and "journalism is a vocation, not something you just stumble into because you don't know what else to do."

Sure, he had been writing for school papers since he could stand with a level of devotion Maebh could never muster, but even he had had career doubts and regretted not doing medicine or law or something that would have made him more money. Foreign affairs had always been his thing but now he was known about town for his food and wine column. Maebh, in truth, hasn't conviction for any profession other than musing about life and books and half suspects that doing anything other than what falls into your lap comes with a kind of gaucheness. And she knows her father is about the same but doesn't realize that getting anywhere these days without contacts is much harder than it was when he walked into a *Toronto Star* job thirty years ago, the day after landing in Canada.

"You should have been an actress," he says, "that was your calling."

'Oh sure!' she thinks. 'I'll get right on that with all the other pretty girls.'

A part of Maebh longs to retreat to the wall again, but she does get an unpaid journalism gig with one of the fellows she interviewed about the Irish band stuff, who is starting an Irish arts and culture magazine on the World Wide Web. She also gets a call from the Hushion Language School with a contract for morning teaching hours. She teaches in the morning for a paycheque and writes in the afternoon about a punk band called Therapy, and on a film about young lovers boating near the Shannon, but she has lost the bloom of first luck. And the fact that she doesn't really know what she's doing or enough about Ireland pop culture or much of anything creeps up over her and she goes silent.

And that's when JC sends another letter asking her to come back. He has a job tarting up old pieces of furniture, Mami has set him up in her old apartment, and school, which starts at age three for Ailis, is right around the corner

The teaching hours increase and Maebh is now making a full-time income but half of it goes to pay for Ailis's daycare which makes moving out on her own impossible and leaves her—a nuisance, and a second-class citizen—at home, sponging off her parents .

"Why can't you handle one child?" Mum asks. "I raised four with an alcoholic of my own."

She is right. Dad was often drunk and absent. He never even took out the garbage and one Christmas Eve when he refused to come home with the car, she had dragged a tree up Parliament from King Street to Dundas during an awful Toronto blizzard. Dad did bring home money, most of the time, to pay for above average lodgings, food, clothes and holidays, but that and all the money it takes to run a family is not something Mum seems to appreciate anymore than Dad appreciates all the work Mum does holding us, all the different houses, and his drinking together.

Before Maebh leaves for Paris, she gets sick again or whatever illness she had that won't go away gets worse for a spell and she meets a Doctor of Traditional Chinese medicine. His name is Micky and he's born and bred in Dublin but studied traditional Chinese medicine for years in Beijing. He's there with a girl she has seen about town a few times, also, called Raffaella. Her mother is from Sri Lanka and her father, the man she never talks to, as Maebh later learns, owns a construction company but is high up in the IRA and uses the business as a cover. Raffaella warns Maebh that Tommy is a bit of a womanizer but when he gives her his business card and offers her treatment, she can already see herself on the doctor's table and so she makes her way to his office the very next day.

It's a whitewashed cottage with flower beds in the window on the outskirts of Dublin. Maebh has to take the dart and a bus to get there but is able to read Flaubert's *Sentimental Education* and enjoys every part of the journey. Tommy leads her into the waiting room while he finishes off with an earlier client but assures her with something in his eye that he has the rest of the afternoon for her. There is that tiger balm smell in the air which Maebh can feel lifting some of the heaviness from her lungs and the Krishna Krishna music he has playing is much more charming and soothing than she thought it might be.

Maebh browses through the magazines about spirituality and alternative health spread about on the coffee table, looking up from time to time to admire his bedroom which she catches enough of a glimpse of to divine that it is painted a deep rust with a large gold-framed mirror over the bed, large leafy plants and pinky prints on the bed.

Soon she finds herself rolled up in blankets with a Buddha statue looming over her in the candle light. Gregorian chants are playing and Maebh feels heavenly transformation already. He's what they call a spiritual healer, which means he gets to place his hands all over her, discreetly but deliberately, and the heat off of them spreads about in circles. He puts little needles in her legs and arms and head and upper chest and gently explains why, but Maebh's too far gone to absorb any specifics. She nods when he tells her that she lets go of inhibitions quickly and how much this will improve her chances of benefiting from the treatment.

She comes back the next day for the same and it is then that she feels herself glowing like the candles. And it is after this treatment that he leads her to his bedroom where he rubs her in oils and drapes her in scarves and makes love to her in the dim orange Ikea lamp she promises to buy for herself one day.

She's wrapped up in these sensations every afternoon the rest of the week and returns home gazing out at the sea from the Dart train with *Sentimental Education* open on her lap. It's just love, a general love, not specific to her or anyone but she idealizes this experience as easily as Flaubert's hero does. Tommy makes sure she knows it is a temporary affair but he never does charge her for the treatment and buys a bottle of Veuve Clicquot to celebrate and she drinks the sparkles like it was her last day on earth. She finds that she's even guilty of touching strangers around her gently on the shoulder a bit more than necessary, as if in passing she is blessing them herself.

She feels perforated with tiny holes waving carefree past the weight of time and space. And by the time she gets on the plane to rejoin a husband for round two of failed marriage, this time with vows broken and expecting much less than the little she expected the first time, she's overcome with healing or is it indifference?

"School will be free there," she says, taking Ailis reassuringly by the hand on the plane.

She looks down upon the layers and layers of thick clouds and imagines that if the plane were to crash, she'd jump out and covet every minute of the descent through cloud and sea. She'd hold Ailis, precious like the cloud whites, to her person.

"Look at those gorgeous green fields," she tells Ailis as the fog dissipates. "All tiny—so many different greens framed by stone fences. We will miss those."

Moving through the thinning cobwebs of water, air and all she idealizes, Maebh's sentimental education proceeds.

18

The front win•ow has a broken pane
someone from Regents Park coul• get blame•
but it was Dad knocking down the hallway.

He took a sle•ge hammer to the front rooms.
"It will feel more spacious."
Then he went back to his
goat cheese and gooseberry jam
and the New York Times.

Beams, old plaster and lath
Jamie crawling in the debris.

Beauty comes from the mess someone else cleans up.

"The Soviets just inva•e• Afghanistan".
His thumbs smudged with ink,
his voice soft, even satisfie•,
but he has terrible dreams.

Maebh sits up on the third bunk
with books she has already read.
The Secret Gar•en an• Anne of Green Gables.
She picks her nose till there's blood
to rub on the bed posts.

Still,
till the shock of hair fills her un•erpants
an• she is strippe• of neutrality.

One summer day,
the living room painted mid blue,
against the drooping benjamina.

The kitchen table is set for
the pink beet soup
they wouldn't eat
but Mum is in bed.

Dad comes by
then the yelling starts and
the dull thumps with his shoes.

"Maebh, call the police!" Mum screams.

He gets like that.
Maybe the whiskey
but violence is a thing on it's own.

His feet ha• once kicke• up all
the toys in their bedroom
when Sinead was still wearing diapers.

It's the only discipline he knows
and he had almost blamed Mum
for asking him to enforce it.

Maebh makes her way up the hallway
and almost gets to their bedroom.
The stairs to the phone are just past the door.

In a few years, he will kick Sinea•
when she comes home at 4 a.m.
Mum waiting up.

"How coul• you •o this to me?"

They ha• never notice• how late she ha• been out before.

"Cal, stop!"

Maebh doesn't talk to boys she loves
or call the cops.
She knows sending Dad to jail
would make her the bad guy.

Da• hea•s off
shoes dragging
but •oesn't check himself in.

An• Mum never calls herself.

19

The recession is in full swing in Europe. Those at the top are pushing down to maintain the appearance they have what they had and those down the ladder are now living in a bachelor apartment, which, though it has its own kitchen and toilet, is smaller than the spare bedroom at Maebh's parents' house. JC's new apartment is the one his grandmother bought with her second husband from Napoli who was much older and died years ago. She was a cleaning lady and he, a truck driver. It is, however, one thing to be sharing a bed-couch with a kid in the living room five minutes from Le Moulin Rouge, and another, on the other side of the Périphérique, in the suburb of Mairie de Clichy. There are no birds over the Montmartre Cemetery for Ailis to look out at but a car mechanic's. HLM Government housing towers, like the one Mami now lives in, sit in pastel-coloured clusters. Poor but tidy is her motto and this place is that—so is Mami, who is delighted to have them so close by and over for Sunday lunch.

"It matches your blouse," Maebh says handing her a peach begonia as she lets them in.

"But it's your birthday!" she says to Maebh setting the begonia on the coffee table in the wrapper so her friends know it's a gift. She ushers them to the dining table right beside it which is stuffed in the middle of the main room between a couch, two armchairs and a large hutch.

"It's nice and cool here Mami!" Maebh says. "Much better than our place." It's been a hot summer in Paris and they have been drinking mint tea with the curtains shut to bear it.

"Ailis and I tried to hide in the ice cream section of the supermarket before coming here!" JC says, sitting her by the begonia with her crayons.

"*Ma petite chérie*!" Mami says, but Ailis scowls at her. "Is she sick?" Mami asks.

"No, no!" Maebh says, embarrassed but also a touch proud that Ailis doesn't like people till they have earned her trust. 'That will protect her,' Maebh thinks, 'from falling for the JC types of this world.'

"Shall we have Campari?" asks Mami clapping her hands.

"In the naked lady glasses?" JC says.

"They aren't naked till you have drunk everything in them," Mami giggles.

"Look!" JC shows me, "dressed on the outside but not on the inside."

"So cute!" Maebh says locking eyes with the blushing woman before Mami fills up the glass.

"Sit down!" she says. "I got sardines from the market this morning and I have a little gift for later."

"Oh Mami, please tell us about your German lover during the war?" JC says.

"He had a beautiful coat," she says.

"Mami favours a sartorial man even when he's the leader of the Front National," JC says winking at her.

"I only voted for him once," she says. "They come here from Africa, fill up the metro seats with kids and won't put the little one on their lap to let me sit down."

"Nobody gives up their seat to anybody, " JC says. "I certainly don't!"

"Colonialism wouldn't make me want to share a seat either!" Maebh says, but Mami's gone off to the kitchen. Maebh pops a small sardine in her mouth with a bit of bread and black olive and enjoys how the salty flavours offset the Campari.

"Look what I bought!" she says, coming out in her sky high heels with a bottle of red wine vinegar that has been over advertised on TV.

"But how wonderful it is to eat off the fat of the land!" sings JC, mocking the commercial.

Mami sprinkles a bit of vinegar on the salad and then leaves the bottle to showcase by the olives as if she has planned this out beforehand. She wouldn't normally be able to afford anything you'd see on TV and the vinegar brings some glamour into her life.

"And how is your new job at the Rock Cafe?" she asks.

"Hard Rock Cafe," JC says laughing.

"I get home at 3 a.m. and Ailis wakes at 8," she says.

"*Pauvre chérie*!" she says.

"But I get some teaching hours next week and they will have a full schedule for me come September. I'm also going to set myself up as a self-employed teacher. My friend Nick does that and makes much more that way. Then when Ailis is settled at school, I'll get my own apartment."

Maebh realizes too late that the Campari is having its effect on her, and that she has said too much about a future that doesn't include JC. JC doesn't seem to have picked up on it but Mami has, and when Maebh gets up to bring dishes into the kitchen, she hears Mami tell JC to make sure his wife doesn't take the new fridge when she leaves.

Mami hands them the paper hats she brought over a few years ago for her birthday and those roll-up horns. Ailis keeps blowing hers and clapping her hands. Maebh blows hers, too, and with more gusto than she expected. She eats her white wine chicken with potatoes, the cheese, salad and cake with relish, quietly plotting her life which, on her twenty-seventh birthday, she's less convinced is utterly ruined, than she was on her twenty-sixth.

"And what about your job, Jean-Christophe?" Mami asks, resting her hand on the wooden chair he painted green and ornate gold for her.

"Kaput!" he says.

—

Ailis loves the little kitchen set and toy bikes the first day of school but kicks and screams every morning the next week. She had just started stringing together some English sentences in Ireland and has now been thrown back into French. She will be silent a few more months before she finally starts talking rather perfectly in French round Christmas at three and three-quarters years old. Not that JC and Maebh are worried. They don't know that's late.

One Friday morning when Ailis seems settled at school, JC offers to show Maebh the bourgeois part of Clichy so they take a little stroll along the Boulevard Gambetta to the park which has the most beautiful pigeons she has ever seen. There's a good boulangerie there and a health food shop and Maebh doesn't have teaching hours till Monday so she picks up a baguette.

"Let's get some milk," JC says. "I don't want that soya crap in my coffee!"

So they stop at Monoprix on their way back.

"I'll get some British marmalade too," she says.

"So you can dunk it on toast in your café au lait," he says teasing her.

She searches through the rows of jams and chooses the Robertsons thick-cut orange, lemon and lime and notices a young woman looking at her—dark eyes, full figure, luminous skin. At the cash, she sees her talking to JC.

"She's as beautiful as the photo!" the woman says.*"Félicitations!"* and slumps out in her sneakers.

Maebh wonders who she is but JC is chatting on about the Robert Musil book he is reading and Maebh notices how much less insightful she finds his thoughts. Has he gotten dumber? Too much booze? Or maybe she's starting to understand that there's more to life than having hours everyday to read *A Man Without Qualities*—that that is what JC has become. Maebh is now disillusioned with books which have brought nothing which might help her cope better with reality. She couldn't even finish *Anna Karenina*—something about the great Tolstoi started bothering her.

"I do love our mini kitchen," she says unpacking the groceries.

JC has made an effort to make them feel welcome. He had painted the kitchen a textured Tuscan rose and had picked up a few white and blue printed dishes at Les Puces to match all the ones he had smashed many years before. And they work well in the kitchen together. Maebh heats up the oven and cuts the baguette into long tartines for toasting while JC makes the coffee.

"One more spoonful—ah yes *comme ça,*" he says. "Don't pat it in!"

"I wish I did things with such flourish," she says watching how his long arms curl about him as he lays the metal *cafetière* on the stove top.

"Ha! Ha!" he says. "It's the French *je ne sais quoi.*"

She puts marmalade and butter onto little plates and sets them out with the bowls for the coffee by the yellow roses she bought a week ago that are pretty though almost dead.

"*Ah! C'est jolie ça!*" he says and she's happy he noticed.

"Breakfast is my favourite," she says.

JC picks up *Libération* which features an article on Jean-Luc Godard.

"Your favourite director," he says with a wink. "He's got a new film out—it's a self-portrait."

"His women are beautiful vapid male-destroying creatures," Maebh says.

"You know some feminists call him their hero."

And then he looks up from the paper with a pointed look on his face as if he has something to tell her. And she thinks this might be a good time to have that conversation about getting a separation and figuring out how to raise Ailis together.

"I went on a date with that girl in the supermarket," he says.

"Oh!"

"She came here and was nice but then she saw your picture and asked about you."

"I'm sorry!" she says.

"She said she couldn't compete with a fashion model."

"Did she really get a look at me?" she asks.

Maebh puts a lump of butter on her bread and some of the bitter marmalade.

"And what about you?" he asks.

"What about me?'

"Did you date anyone in Ireland while you were home?"

Her mind goes back to those afternoons with silky scarves.

"You slut!" he says reading her face and there's that irrationality in his eyes she can't attach to the man she thinks he should be.

"No more than you," she says looking at the marmalade which stirs like a molten jewel.

"So how did it go?"

He picks up *Libération* again and rifles through the pages like he doesn't care. It's a left-wing libertine type newspaper, the kind evolved men are supposed to read but Godard looks indifferent.

"It just happened!" Such a welcome break, she thinks, from feeling abandoned and having to pay for everything.

"It?" he asks.

"I didn't orgasm with him either," she says, but thinks about how beautifully Tommy had touched her all the same.

JC puts the paper down quietly and then slaps her on the face like he hasn't since that time when they first arrived in Paris.

"Godard was right! *Tu es vraiment une dégueulasse!*" he says. "All of you—I'm done with you!"

"Godard can go to hell!" Maebh says. Her face is stinging.

JC puts on his jacket like he's going to leave.

"So who was the lucky guy?" he says turning back.

"Just some quack acupuncture doctor," she says. But he had gotten rid of her chest infection, or maybe feeling cared for did, she thinks.

"So that's where you got those China pills from," he says rushing over to the cupboard where she's stored the ginseng and whipping it out the window into the garage below.

"Heh!" the mechanics yell up at them.

Then JC comes over and slaps her again but this time he clutches his hands and it's more like a punch.

Maebh puts her hand on her face in disbelief.

"But we were separated," she says. There's coffee everywhere burning through her dress. The toasts are all mushy and they could just have enjoyed their breakfast and been good parents together.

But JC jumps up and down smashing the walls like a gargoyle caricature. He seems to have almost forgotten she's there and or even what he's angry about but then comes back at her as she moves slow side-steps towards the front door.

"I've brought you nothing but unhappiness!" Maebh says.

He swings his arms more wildly like the universe is his enemy and she's sure she does get a few more thumps but it's not that which has seized her but the look in his eyes. She stares into them looking for something reasonable but then bows her head like an animal in submission and backs out slowly from the apartment. Little breath, calm breath. It's almost intoxicating, the terror that comes from knowing how very small she is in his eyes—that she has no self for him, that she never had, that what he demands of her, he never has of himself, that he has always denied her existence so it's easy to now want her gone.

He follows her down the stairs. She spreads her energy out evenly through her feet at each step using every ballet muscle—sure he would never actually claim to wanting her to fall but would blame her and not himself for his inexplicable temper if it were to happen. She walks backwards with tight sliding grip on the bannister, all the way down smaller and smaller and closer into herself but determined to keep him at bay, however strangely he looks at her throat. Like he wants to put his hands round it! And by the time she gets to Mami's apartment she has become but a shadow too fluid to have mass.

He kicks and pushes Maebh now viciously as he can and tells Mami what a whore she is, but Mami, despite her German soldier lover and kitschy naked lady paintings, could never be on Maebh's side. Maebh gets on the other end of the table and they circle round together. She stares at his twitching hands. She can feel them on her neck even from a distance which is the only thing protecting her and the fact that JC is so angry he has almost lost all coordination. Maebh has only a weak sense of shape and perspective but she somehow stays out of his way, knowing that he would choke her physically now if he could as he has been emotionally these years. And only then does she see this so clearly, she almost sighs in relief as it is in the moment that he most has her under his clutches that she finally loses respect for him and this gives her some strength.

"Get out of here!" Mami says afraid her place is about to be wrecked.

So Maebh slips out, all ears, when she hears people in the hall waiting for the elevator. She can feel JC near her. His anger is fading but she keeps people between them as they go down.

She goes to Ailis's school which is right around the corner and the only other place where people who know her to be a sane and decent person might protect her. He doesn't follow her in and when she looks back to see him standing there she doesn't see a monster but a dejected creature—wild and heart-breaking. But maybe that is her.

She collects Ailis and orders a taxi from the school, and when she's in it, on her way to Djamila's, they drive right by the police station and she wonders why she doesn't go in but then she can't fathom what has happened. His eyes! His hands! She holds Ailis on her knee under her seat belt. They stare at the passing evening lights all blurred and vacant one into the other.

When she gets to Djamila's she thinks she might collapse but Djamila is on the phone with JC. "He's left 15 messages!" she whispers. "He says he put all your stuff on the street because you didn't come home." She puts the phone on speaker.

"I'm sorry," he says. "Still it's what she deserves," he laughs.

"Why?" Maebh says. Her heart tears again.

"What have you done JC?" Djamila says leading Maebh gently to the couch where she sits holding Ailis like she never wants to move. "I never expected you to be such a conservative shit!"

"Yeah, you are right!" he says, "I went back to get everything but someone had taken it already."

Djamila's cat rubs against Maebh's leg.

"Just tell her to come back," he says.

"I mean what woman, or man for that matter, would put up with you?" Djamila says.

"I'm done and am heading out of town," he says. "So that *pouffiasse* can have the apartment."

—

Maebh does go back again. Not right away but on Sunday. Djamila drives them home.

"My poor little tin-can car is on its last legs," she says struggling to re-adjust the rearview mirror which comes loose in her hands.

"I love this car!" Maebh says.

"I haven't been able to get any film work since the recession or since I turned thirty," she says.

"You need to make your own film," Maebh says.

"And you need to get your own place," Djamila says.

"Ailis just got used to school and JC's gone to Besançon," she says. "And I have to teach on Monday."

They walk through the Clichy apartment which looks the same except the closet is empty.

"There's nothing left of me," Maebh says. She moves cautiously looking for something he might have missed. Her vintage pink cashmere turtleneck and black wool coat with the velvet trim—all gone. Her books and CDs are there but they became his as soon as he touched them. The Arvo Pärt is open on the shelf and she can almost hear it streaming through the room.

"I'm done with stuff!" Maebh says. "Or stuff is done with me!"

"Where did all his anger come from?" Djamila asks.

Maebh had listened with every animal sense to his voice on the phone just before he left, trying to uncover his motives. He had sounded so normal no one would have imagined he could have taken his rage so far, and though JC had always been a walking red card, assessing not how one is everyday but how one is in a moment of crisis is easier said than done.

They move into the bathroom but the Nivea cream is gone and all her makeup and shampoo. Maebh has disappeared there too except she sees her face in the mirror and her fingers, and she's wearing the Emanuel Ungaro shirt dress Mum gave her a few years ago It's a bit big and she looks over-dressed often even on the weekend. It's her shell and one way of hiding her wretchedness. She doesn't own or didn't own jeans or what they call lounge clothes. She can't wear them to work so they would have been a luxury.

—

A few months later, and a bit after JC calls to say he is coming back in a few weeks, she finds—walking by the Clichy Town Hall—an apartment to rent. He had spoken like a normal man doing normal man stuff but she has known she needs to move out for some time but had been too busy to find anything so this place seems to be there just for her. It is up on the top floor overlooking the new square which has recently been planted with trees and benches and other green things over what was once the Town Hall car park. The *For Rent* sign seems to be waving at her and looking up she feels the claustrophobia round her lessen, so she copies down the number to see it.

On her way to the viewing, she smooths her ponytail and adjusts the badly fitting pants she just bought without trying on first. The apartment is in a well-maintained building with red carpet up the stairs and a 1920's elevator. However, the carpets, in what will become her apartment, are stained and puckering and the whole place needs a paint job. The kitchen is a half fridge with a two-element stovetop and has thick oily splashes up the wall but Maebh only sees the large south facing windows looking out over the square, and that it is twice the size of the studio she was sharing with JC, so she decides to take the place right away. She calculates that with a monthly rent help cheque she'll be able to make it work and social services gives her the deposit to secure the place. The apartment has been unoccupied for some time but the sunshine streaming in through the white lace curtains hides some of its sadness.

"The owners were trying to sell it but nobody wanted it," the agent said.

'Except me!' Maebh thinks.

Ailis and she step over to the window, where they can see the tips of the Eiffel Tower to the right and Sacré-Coeur to the left clear over the roofs of suburban Paris.

"You have a window to look out of again, my beautiful Ailis," Maebh says glad there are bars stretched across the lower half to keep her from falling.

Maebh's parents drive to visit with a small table and some beautiful dishes that Granny had decided to part with. She knows they are precious but is now indifferent to anything material. Her finger gently traces the six pink flowers round each dish as if she is trying to remember something. Dad comes by reluctantly to help her move Ailis's toys and things at Mum's insistence but Mum has a headache.

Maebh leaves the books and stereo she paid for. She does think about taking the second tome of Proust she never got a chance to finish but she is done with books. She leaves the furniture and the lousy fridge but brings a bit of cutlery. It all fits in one half garbage bag of stuff which Dad dumps on the table in the new place beside the flowered dishes. He says the apartment is nice and rushes off.

Maebh wishes she had asked him to take her to get a mattress but she forgot so she and Ailis sleep on the floor that week till she gets one delivered. She also wishes that he and Mum had offered to help her paint but she's years away from expecting anything substantial from people. Besides her parents fed her and Ailis all last year and are tired of her problems and Maebh doesn't blame them. She swerves the table corner by corner over to the window and puts the two wooden fold-up chairs they brought with it one at each end. Then she sets up the dishes on the kitchen counter. They are too pretty in fact and Granny knew she'd be the only one who'd want them. She unrolls the rag rug that used to sit in Granny's spare bedroom over the big stain on the carpet right in the middle of the room and then she goes to pick up Ailis from school.

—

"I always knew you would sneak off like that," JC says when he calls. "You even took the can opener."

"That's all I took," she says.

His voice sounds like some far away version of itself and Maebh sounds perhaps too cheerful. Later when she goes down to meet him in the park, he has one leg beautifully crossed over the other on a bench but his dejection is obvious. Ailis runs to cuddle in his lap and Maebh does what she can to lift his spirits. She wonders why her voice falls into a nurturing tone but she sees no signs of the man who clobbered her a few months ago and threw out all her possessions.

"Nothing will change—you can see Ailis everyday!" she says and then she even lets him come up to see the place.

There is something so calming about the light that comes in and the possibilities that might fill two empty rooms. They eat the rest of some soup Maebh made and she's convinced that if she can make everything seem normal, maybe it will be.

"We can raise Ailis together but we can't live together," she says after Ailis falls asleep and then she lies with him and undresses him like a baby and kisses his naked body goodbye as many times as she can but more like a mother soothing than a wife. He looks at her and mistakes her lightness for a sense he might still have her. His body's fragile confusion touches her and she does do everything she can to comfort him and rock him into an acceptance of their situation. She wants tenderness to cure all.

The phone rings when he's getting dressed. It's Nick, her English teacher friend—the masculine in his voice somehow coming through very loud in the empty room and the fact that he does fancy her and it is 10 p.m., so JC is all of a sudden a seething other creature again. He moves into the kitchen where the pink flower dishes are carefully stacked on the countertop with bottles of oil, vinegar, tomato sauce and jam. Maebh runs to get Ailis before the smashing begins but there is no time to get out so she locks the bedroom door and sits with her back against it and her hand on the phone till she hears his angry steps rush out the door and down the stairs.

She calls Djamila and gets her to wait on the other end while she searches the place—pink china and tomato sauce are smashed everywhere on the kitchen floor.

"Why did you let him in?" she asks clearly annoyed.

"He's gone," Maebh can barely speak so she hangs up.

—

The next morning sunshine pours through the windows. It's market day and Maebh can hear the bustle through the windows she has left crossed over each other the way you do to let a bit of breeze in. The wine merchants in the shop across the square tell you which wine and at what price to pair with Boeuf Bourguignon and she tries to think of these things as she waits in a body that might never move again for Ailis to wake up.

"Where's Daddy?" Ailis says with a smile.

"He's at his house," she says. "And we live here now."

Ailis nods as if that is how it should be.

They slept fully dressed so getting up is easier and they go out straight. Maebh closes the door on the kitchen floor and they take the stairs softly down. Ailis is as instinctively quiet as her mother who gives her a few digestive biscuits and some raisins from the bottom of her purse for breakfast.

"Would you like *un chocolat chaud?*" she asks.

"Chocky chaud, chocky chaud!" Ailis beams so sweetly Maebh has to hide her tears, which is easy because they don't actually transpire.

Ailis has a free hot lunch at school so Maebh knows she will have a proper meal in a few hours. They walk to her school hand in hand. The market sellers fill the street with baskets of vegetables, odd kitchen supplies and someone is roasting chickens on a rotating spit and stuffing them in bags with sauce and frites.

"Would you like one of those for dinner?" Maebh says.

But Ailis says, "Daddy is nice to me but not to you Mummy!"

Maebh sees a bit of pride and a reproach when she looks down at her.

"I know!" Maebh says and swings her up into her arms to hug her. It's such a relief Ailis understands but Maebh knows she will miss her father and that Maebh will likely miss him too. Ailis pushes away as she often does when Maebh hugs too much and too long. Maebh stares into the blue in her eyes, like hers, but with a darker surety and wonders where she got it.

They come up to Ailis's school and Ailis runs in gaily as she always does. Maebh feels she is safest there and can't imagine straying from the usual routine however surreal their situation— or maybe it isn't. People try to destroy each other all the time. It can happen willingly or by happenstance. It is hard to govern your own emotions and it is hard to bring out the best in another or in oneself. There is some kind of chemistry that happens between people and finding someone who sets off a healthy reaction is not easy to recognize even if you find it. You aren't given a manual when you have a baby and you aren't given one when you find a husband either.

Maebh cleans up the dishes and condiments from the kitchen floor but tries not to think about them or the shoes, sweaters, creams and things swept up from the curb when JC threw them out. She leans up against the wall in the kitchen when all the larger pieces have been collected and there's just a layer of oily red on the tile with mini shards of glass. She lets the pin pricks of cruelty sink through but she doesn't cry till she notices she's cut her finger and she won't ever remember exactly how she gets rid of the rest of the mess. Tiny swirls of glass and sticky mess get stuck in between the tiles. She thinks she must have used a small piece of cardboard paper to scoop it up. A black is taking over her mind but it's a black she buries within her better this time.

They are only dishes and it's not like he pounded her head with them. But who is she without them? These things are more than themselves and if someone strips you of them, it is as if to say you can exist but are not to live for yourself with any of the trappings—the trappings that clothe your soul. And you understand that a soul is nothing without a proper shape defined for it, that it needs to be clothed, and that if that person pretending to love you wants you to live without these things it is because he never wanted you to live for yourself—as a defined being— but only for him.

Maebh tries to get ready for work but there's grey thickness, too thick to wade through, so she decides to stay home. She has been teaching all this time and the grey has been there for years and she could make it but calls and says she can't. No one asks why but she feels it, this why, why is this happening, and the need to hide it from her voice.

"Okay, I'll let your students know."

And that's it. She sleeps on and off and might never get up again except she does to get Ailis.

—

Ailis has nightmares a black stallion is trying to kill her.

"I'm afraid to die Mummy," she says.

"You aren't going to die Ailis," Maebh says gently stroking her cheeks.

"But how do you know?" she asks. Her eyes are too intelligent for a fuzzy answer that could never comfort so Maebh doesn't give one.

"Well, death is a mystery and you can't really predict it but you are young and healthy, Paris is very safe and your Mummy takes good care of you so it's not likely you will die for a very long long time".

"But I might!"

"Shsh! Shsh! Shsh!" Maebh says holding her tight till she falls back asleep because she doesn't know what else to say and the usual panic at how she has failed her is rising up her throat.

On the weekend, Maebh takes Ailis to Notre Dame.

"Some people don't believe we ever die. They think that we go to a place called heaven with angel wings and beautiful golden fields."

"Do you believe that?" Ailis asks.

"I don't think I do but I do think coming to this place can make you feel safe and closer to God."

"If there is a God."

"Right and if there is a God, you can try talking to him when you feel bad. Maybe you are really only talking to yourself or some other force up there but it can help." Maebh gestures up at the high stone arches overhead.

Ailis looks up with her eyes impressed and heads off down the far left aisle of the church with her hands behind her back. Smaller than the pews, she stares at the beauty and cruelty in the stained glass windows and feels the echoes around her. Then she turns back and walks past them again.

"Help me give her a better life!" Maebh whispers.

"The stories are terrible!" Ailis says but it's like the place has removed both their terrors.

They walk out the Cathedral and Maebh picks up Ailis to show her how to dip her finger in the urn of holy water and make the sign of the cross.

"It can protect you!" she says.

A few days later, Maebh decides to go to the police. She knows worse things are happening in the world but she signs a document to say she and JC have separated and tells the officer he kept taking swipes at her and all the rest with the clothes and dishes but she can't remember with what fist or where or how many exactly. She can't remember what clothes she had nor did she ever know what corner he left them on or on what date these things all happened. The officer takes notes and nods but avoids looking at her and she wonders if it was even worth reporting.

They can't fix it, she thinks, but if JC does it again there is a trace. At least she has articulated the crime deep within herself and decided it shouldn't be happening because he does do it again, and worse, but not to her.

A few months from now, a woman he dates will contact her. He slammed her down, she writes, and dug his hands into her throat strangling her till her older son pulled him off. Maebh won't respond with true sympathy but will think this woman silly for goading him on, for not walking on eggshells like her, which is not fair—not even to her own self.

The police officer is evasive until Maebh explains it happened not in the matrimonial home but in her own apartment paid for by her. She had paid rent and food for "the family" for years but a woman is nothing within the grip of marriage.

"How do you say your name?" the police officer says staring at the form she has just completed.

"Mais Eve Murray", she says. He runs his eyes up her person—quirky tan shoes, grey work trousers and green patterned 70's style clingy blouse. It's Granda's tweed cap backwards on her head which gives her away.

"You aren't British are you?" he says.

"I'm Irish!" she says, knowing this is what he wants to hear. He nods in satisfaction as if being Irish explains why a born and bred Frenchman would lower himself to such things. She could have said Canadian and defied his expectations but knows it is the worst of Irish cliché which has her here and watching him confirm that was too tempting.

A few weeks later, she sees JC standing near Ailis's school. She had been afraid of that. What if he left town with her? But he is wavering in his shoes. He looks desperate and the school hadn't let him take her. They obviously recognize these things better than Maebh does. She doesn't talk or go near him and he doesn't seem capable of more than staring at her like it's all her fault.

He leaves Paris for good this time. Staying is a too painful representation of his failure or perhaps he is afraid of what he might do or is that something Maebh wants to believe. So now she is alone with Ailis who bounces beside but knows not to go over to her father and holds her hand just a little bit tighter than usual. The guilt Maebh traces back and forward grows deeper— what a father she has given this child and what a mother too.

20

Orpheus turns back to his wife
If he •oes not look he •oes not love
and love he must.

If he •oes not look he •oes not see
and see he must.

A man is not a man
if he •oes what he shoul• but what he woul•
an• what he woul• is something set of him.

What is set of him
opens him to a kin• of unpacking,
an or•ering of things from within.

This is the human dilemma.

Maebh is she who plummets down
but Orpheus as well.

They are married in her
and to understand that sum
She marries the man she does.

She stepped into the void
to know the suffering
she had not recognized.

This marriage will tell her
of all marriages

This chil•hoo• of all
childhoods

The details brushed out
in a larger common ache

Fathers, mothers, children,
loved, neglected, never understood.

She grasps hold as she grasps the tree in Prague.

The husband draped round her,
too •runk to stan• or ever care for another
overwhelme• by himself.

He will drape the chains
to decipher.

The lyre of Orpheus plays on
and Eurydice hurtles back to the abyss.
The love in their last look more
than they have ever known.

She will try but never love this husband like that nor he her
but she will watch the many pointe• si•es of herself
—the si•es lost to sha•e—
till they are more loved than hated
and she is one.

21

She takes the metro to different locations in Paris every morning. After, that is, she drags herself out of bed, forces clothes onto and food into Ailis and takes her to school, where she knows with great relief she will be happy. Parents do this everyday all over the globe but it does Maebh in. Wavering in her shoes as the train goes by on the metro platform she holds a placard. It says; let the earth open up and take me away. Maebh is not sure where that might be but somewhere less harsh. She teaches all over Paris as she did before—marketing managers, engineers, and people who manage logistics—and years later, their jobs make as little sense to her as ever. Some companies pay her half of what she's owed because she could never count her hours worked. Her paycheque is somehow enough to cover the bare necessities and she can't think beyond that.

She finds a way to make a home—a beat up green velvet armchair and a click-clack couch bed from some Scottish students leaving the city that she covers with an expensive brown and peachy flowered covering she picks up on sale in Saint-Germain. There's a marble fireplace that doesn't work with a mirror over it against one wall and in the dim light of the plastic orange lamp she picked up with sheets and an armoire at IKEA, the place is lovely if you don't look too close. She's not dressed as well as she used to be and no amount of makeup can give her the glow she once had.

She gives private lessons to Rita from Lebanon who is the only cool-looking mother at Ailis's school. She and her then husband had moved out here to escape the city and save their marriage but it hasn't worked. A month after she meets her, Rita decides she has to get out of the suburbs, and her marriage, and moves with all the other cool people to the eleventh *arrondissement*.

Rita pouffs her hair perfectly and wears mini-skirts with little pointy high heels every day. She looks a bit like Ally McBeal. She invites Maebh to a party in Saint-Cloud, a ritzy suburb at the other end of Paris. Maebh wears a dress from one of the many cheap clothing shops you find in Paris which is reasonably well tailored and 70's style sandals with a higher than her usual heel. She finds herself in conversation with a man in a navy polo shirt and lots of scrunchy fair hair on his arms. He asks her who she knows here and she tells him she's here with her student and unlike other men who fancy her he doesn't make up some story about how he needs an English teacher. They speak a bit more but she's on her second glass of wine and *Arizona Dream* is playing so she dances, which he takes as an invitation; but she insists she'd rather on her own. That's true, though she does smile at him a few times to compensate. There's something frumpy about his polo shirt, but he's so uncommonly nice that when he asks for her number directly, instead of handing her a show-off business card, she gives it to him. She doesn't consider herself a very good judge of character but this man feels safe. Of course, she also gives it to him because she still doesn't know what else to do.

The next morning, the man calls her and tells her that he so enjoyed talking to her that he had to cross town to leave something beautiful at her door. Ailis is watching *Mary Poppins* and playing with the fairy Barbie Maebh couldn't resist buying for her. His voice is gentle so she opens the door without thinking and finds a bouquet of peonies. A dozen of them, the pale pink kind, wrapped in stiff brown paper tied up with straw twine.

"They are so elegant," she says, "but I have to go."

She's suddenly scared and slides down onto the couch wondering how he found her address.

"I'm sorry for alarming you," he says. " I was so taken with you and knew I might never see you again."

Maebh sinks further into the cushions.

"Someone let me into the building and another told me there was an English lady with a small child in the far right apartment on the sixth floor."

"I have to go," she says.

"May I call you tomorrow?" he asks.

He does sound genuine.

"Please!" she says.

Taken with her, she thinks. Someone is taken with her.

And so begins her love affair with a millionaire. He is the CEO of a leading financial company with a head office on the Champs-Élysées and he picks her up in his chauffeur-driven Mercedes. He also gives her more compliments than she's ever had which makes her think Djamila was right in thinking she had never reached high enough.

"You look like a cross between Michelle Pfeiffer and Charlotte Rampling," he says and that only makes her think of the Charlotte Rampling whose fascist husband sent her off to a concentration camp in *The Conformist.*

He talks to her about his divorce and his daughter and how he had seen a healer in Agadez who had said he had ignored the spiritual within himself in favour of great financial success, and Maebh starts thinking perhaps they have something to give each other. He wants to write something creative and she has decided to give books up to make money.

Getting out to meet him is often complicated. On her birthday, she's late because the babysitter forgot to come and she had to walk Ailis to Mami's. He gives her a jade bracelet but because she's not used to gifts and has never worn jewelry she doesn't know how to thank him. So he takes it back and exchanges it for a more expensive dark blue necklace that really doesn't suit her anywhere near as well. He takes her to his apartment that night and a few other nights. It's empty and cold but off a quiet treed courtyard in the fifth *arrondissement* away from the congestion of Paris. They begin sexual relations a few hours, weeks, or even months too early. Maebh takes off her clothes like she is supposed to. Her back arches and she make noises in pretense but his disappointment is palpable and hers is too.

"You aren't attracted to me," he says.

"But I am!"

And she loses him. And a few more. She functions day to day but the thought of being with a man sets on a kind of paralysis.

—

Raising Ailis on her own is as exhausting as raising her with an alcoholic JC—a double shift teaching and taking care of her morning and night. She misses JC's muddled up intellectual discourse and his cooking. Weekends are lonely and absorbed with tiring duties. She can't remember the last time she sat with a book in a café. Even if she does go out in the evening, she has to wake in the morning with Ailis so it doesn't seem worth it. Sometimes she doesn't get her from school till 6 p.m. either because she's teaching late, or if she needs fifteen minutes alone to daydream. Poor Ailis is as cranky and hard to deal with as Maebh. On occasion, she refuses to move and screams in the middle of the sidewalk till Maebh picks her up like a sack of potatoes and carries her furious little body to her bedroom where she leaves her to calm down. Maebh cuts vegetables for soup, and when they are cooked, the droning noise of the Braun mixer synchs with her brain while the pork chops smoke on the pan—sometimes they burn.

Often she feels her frustrations mounting beyond the bearable, trying to get Ailis in and out of the bath—which is really a mouldy shower stall with a plastic tub in it—and asleep in five minutes. She keeps looking at her watch frantically—how fast the minutes pass. Ailis will never wake up for school and then Maebh will be late for work again. Ailis screams so loud during her bath, while her mother tries to comb the conditioning through her curls, and even louder when she threatens to cut it all off. Maebh is seized with anger and her hand, with a weight of its own but representative of every ugly weakness Maebh knows is within her, smacks her daughter as hard as she can. The red mark of Maebh's hand shows itself on Ailis's face. Maebh takes a breath and tries to wrap the little naked body of her child in a towel. The body is convulsing and Maebh apologizes over and over and the body allows herself to be held but refuses eye contact. And why would she when this has happened before when she wouldn't eat the soup or put on warm enough clothes for school.

"I'm so sorry," Maebh says again and Ailis shakes her head, her eyes dark and angry. They walk back and forth together connecting to their mutual confusion till they both stop crying.

Maebh tucks her daughter into bed with her fairy Barbie.

"We all have darkness in us," Maebh tells her as she closes her eyes. "But it's not okay to hit anyone, especially someone smaller than you."

Ailis squeezes her hand the way she does and Maebh's determined more than ever to find a strategy to help curb these outbreaks and she takes out a notebook to make a list of ways to summon a reasonable way out.

"I'm as violent as JC without alcohol as an excuse," she tells Djamila over the phone.

"Yeah! Not cool!" she says.

"More guilty even because I know it's not right."

"Just don't hit her on the head," she says.

"In Canada, they would take her from me."

"Give her a slap on the hand but with a warning first," Djamila says.

"I don't want to hit her at all," Maebh says.

"A little tap is okay but not in anger," Djamila says.

Miraculously this works. When Ailis becomes intolerable Maebh warns her and if she doesn't listen she smacks her little hand gently. Eventually, Maebh no longer needs to smack her palm but tells Ailis she will have to sit in the corner instead. Maebh still has the anger though and does still lose her temper. She reduces her work hours, hires more babysitters and makes sure she gets time to herself. She has less money but the resulting peace is worth it.

"There needs to be twenty-four-hour emergency places you can bring a child when you need a break," she tells Djamila. "It's not like you can remove the batteries from your kid and put them on a shelf till you are a good parent again."

"That would be cool," Djamila says.

"Don't hate me but I get it when I hear of people just up and abandoning their children and even understand parents who take their own lives and the lives of their children too."

"Maybe you should give Ailis to her French grandparents to raise," Djamila says.

"I could never! Besides by loving her, I might even be loving myself".

"You could just do it for six months while you get your life together."

"Ailis spent a few weeks there last spring and came back in a retracted sullen state as if she were traumatized. Anyway, I would miss her too. I just wish caring for her wasn't so non-stop arduous."

"You're a better mother than I could be," Djamila says.

"You don't want children."

"Never! My mother brought us here to escape that."

"I get it!" Maebh says. "A woman is a myriad of many things."

"She can wear any shoes she wants."

"Have you been watching *Sex and the City* again?" Maebh says.

"Actually, I'm making a short film," Djamila says.

"That's great!"

"It's about FGM".

"What's that?"

"Oh, come on white girl!"

"Don't call me white girl! I'm Irish pink remember."

"Which blends with white rather easily! Female Genital Mutilation. It's like circumcision for women."

"What!"

"Yes, when my mother turned fifteen the women came for her one night, held her down and cut off her clitoris."

"Oh my god!"

"And then they had a party and she had to pretend to be happy about all the pain she was in."

"I just can't!" Maebh says. "I don't even know how you recover from that."

"You don't recover. But you do get on with your life or at least that is what the women I'm interviewing say."

"I'm so proud of you."

"Thanks, I just wish I could find more women to talk too and I need to ask the right questions. I don't want to impose too much on them but just let them talk without, you know, saying, tell me about it."

—

JC doesn't come to visit even once but he calls. He has found another older woman in a small village near where his parents live.

"She orgasms every time," he tells her. "And her breasts shake all over the place."

"I'm happy for you!" Maebh says relieved, despite feeling half a woman and nobody's wife, that she doesn't have to worry about him.

JC's girlfriend is good to Ailis and they start to take her a few weeks a year. There are no cars in the village where they live, which rolls up a small hill that hovers over sunflower fields. Lots of children run in the streets. There's a dog to walk and a pond to swim in. It's a kind of little paradise.

Maebh makes more resolutions to improve her life. She eventually sets herself up as a freelancer and makes double on short-term teaching contracts, so she buys a wooden vintage table from Les Puces market, a long grey coat to hide under and a Barbie knapsack for Ailis. She's not too happy about Ailis in her Barbie phase and tries to buy her the ones with wings over the business, slutty ones, but she reasons that Ailis will tire of it quicker if she's indulged and a year later Ailis is done with Barbie.

She keeps trying to improve their place. She doesn't have the energy to paint but tries cleaning the walls which stay mostly dirty but do look a bit less shabby. She files her taxes for the first time and when the woman at the office tells her she hasn't made enough to pay any she feels determined to make more.

"I'm ready to be bourgeois," she tells Ailis later that evening, only partly aware that to some extent she actually is. They are eating the cabbage soup Maebh chopped up and blended. There's more of that leftover roast chicken on a plate and an apple but no milk or cheese. Ailis gets earaches too often and Maebh read that dairy is not good. They have also started eating gluten-free like the rest of the family. Maebh's father, who had switched from whiskey to red wine, had decided that it was this and not the need for psychotherapy at the root of all their problems. Ailis puts *Mary Poppins* on after dinner as they do about once a week. Actually Maebh doesn't usually have time to watch it with her and Ailis dresses up and dances with her umbrella in front of it alone—it helps her keep up her English.

"And I'll pay lots of taxes too!" Maebh says.

"Why?" says Ailis.

"Because France takes care of us."

Djamila has a new man and invites her to dinner.

"He's the most amazing cook," she says. "He's from Brittany."

"So's the crab!" Bertrand says caressing it like it's his baby and then dumping it head first into a huge pot of boiling water. He picks up a small bowl of salt and pinches some into the water with herbs.

"It's okay—my darling," he says. Then he makes an aioli—stirring in the thinnest stream of oil with the egg yolk and garlic all hunched over, but with a steady hand. He flares his nose with satisfaction all of a sudden.

"The crab is ready," and he picks it out of the water with a pair of large spoon things and plonks it on the serving dish on the kitchen table.

"*Quelle beauté*!" he says.

They eat it squished round the table, snapping crab juices and napkins everywhere, with the most perfect bottle of white wine and a simple green salad.

Ailis eats it too. She loves gourmet food and Maebh had caught her eating all the caviar off the canapés at a Christmas party in Dublin.

"It's the best meal I've ever had!" Maebh says. "And you, Bertrand, are the cutest most cliché Frenchman I've ever met."

"Why thank you!" he says. "Then I must continue with these clichés and tell you about the book I've been reading while I smoke my Gitanes," he laughs. He scoops a big bit of soft chèvre onto a teeny bit of baguette and devours it in one gulp before lighting his cigarette, the ashes of which he will flick with great flourish onto his plate.

"White man is more corrupt and evil than any other," he announces.

"I don't know!" Maebh says. "Tell that to Kubla Khan."

"No comparison!" Bertrand says.

"I just think there is a kind of fake humility in such a statement—it's in our nature—like a get out of jail free card and kind of gives one license to continue."

"What do you mean?"

"Maybe saying someone is made to be worse is almost like saying they are made to be better?"

"Hmn!" Bertrand says.

"It's like how we say women are too sweet for this or that and Wall Street, and that keeps them away from it and men in control of it."

"Interesting!" Bertrand says dumping the stack of dinner dishes with knives, forks, cigarette butts and crab shells in the sink.

"But all the same 'white man' has much to answer for and the 'liberal' ones at the top should look hard at themselves," adds Djamila who has her yellow gloves on and is picking delicately through the fishy tobacco shells, so Maebh joins her, holding open the bin for them, wondering as she often does, where this outburst, about a book she hasn't even read, has come from.

"He doesn't do dishes or cook vegetables but he ripped through my lace blouse on our third meeting," she laughs. Maebh notices that she has another new dress and has been very attentive with her hair recently but still doesn't wear any makeup. She glows more than ever and doesn't need to.

"He's really cool!" Maebh says. She takes Ailis into the bedroom to get her to fall asleep and comes back an awkward while later with Ailis still awake in her arms.

"I went to see an astrologer," Djamila says giving Maebh a why-are-you-letting-that-kid-control-you look. "He's famous for treating many of France's leading entertainers. You know, I haven't been able to find a job in film production for years and he said I should make my own."

"Wow, and you are making your own!" Maebh says.

"But there's no money in it!"

"Who needs money?" And Djamila gives her another pointed look.

"He also told me that being beautiful, educated and from a good family is not enough. That I'm looking for more."

—

Maebh has never seen astrology as more than something to read on the subway while bored but finds herself calling to make an appointment and liking the mix of mystery and humour she hears in the astrologer's slightly affected baritone. She's so intrigued that she calls him back a few minutes later to change her appointment for the earlier one he proposed.

"Aha! I'll see you in two days then," he says with triumph. "You are obviously ready to see me."

Louis runs his office out of his apartment near the Jardin du Luxembourg. He has a round odd face as expressive as his voice with thin dark hair slicked back. Maebh learns that he was an actor and playwright with La Comédie Française and is now a theatre director. He leads her into his waiting-room as if he has planned the entrance carefully, removes her coat and appraises her person.

"I expected you to be a little more generous in the figure though Madame," he says and seats her at one of the many grey leather couches to wait. "I won't be long with this client—he is, unfortunately, only a man!"

In his office, she sits at his desk and his indiscreet charm makes her laugh quite a few times. There is something about him which seeks to seduce almost as if it is his duty. This is a very French habit but he seems to have mastered it better than most and in such an entertaining way, she overlooks his creepier aspects. Maebh also ignores too the round belly, receding hairline and large spaced out teeth because he's attractive all the same and seems so anxious to help her. But she had felt that even before meeting him, given the jauntiness of her steps along the metro platform.

"You know how to survive but not how to live," he says peering at her with deep concern. "You are a myth of your own creation stuck in false ideas of what it means to be 'good' but not a heroine carving out her destiny. You desired your father as a small child and he desired you and this has made you guilty and frigid and afraid of men. There are brutes, lambs and beasts or the abuser, self-centred wimp and a real man who is not afraid to show his desire but doesn't get angry if you don't return it. A real man who has a heart but is not afraid to show his passion so he takes you in his arms."

He keeps talking on and on in this way without asking her a question or letting her speak a single word.

"You confuse sex and love all the time!" he says and now he is chiding her. "What a pain in the ass you are—all these lovers coming in and out of your life! When a man is even just the tiniest bit nice, you take off your clothes but don't always enjoy it."

"If only my father and I had been able to hug," she says the weirdness would have gone away.

"*Oui, c'est ça*!", he says. "The touch of a parent is different from the touch of a lover and you need to learn that as children."

"I see," she says.

"Finally, you are a writer."

"No, I'm not!"

"*Oui, ma chérie!*" he says. "You have something to say, the world needs to hear what you have to say and you know how to say it. But it's going to be hard for you and I don't know if you will be able to manage it. You need to completely change your life and it's going to take every bit of strength you have to do it. Fortunately, you have it in you to take this challenge on. You enjoy putting yourself in masochistic situations. Isn't that true?" he says.

"Well it is!" she says.

"You are suffering!" he says. "And I want to help you. Come here every week and we'll see what we can do."

She asks him how much it will all cost.

"Ah yes!" he says. "You have financial stresses as well so just bring me whatever you can. A pack of Lucky Strikes even. Astrology was made for people like you. You have power. More power than you know how to handle and that frightens you. It would be an honour to work with you."

She leaves his office with a sense of validation or jubilation—"an honour!" But she's also confused.

"If I'm a writer, why haven't I?" she will ask him. "And I'm lonely!"

"Pff!" he will say. "Don't be pathetic!"

"Perhaps the writing is in the same dried up state as my sexuality?"

"The woman who writes will find her husband and not the other way round. And with him she will find sexual fulfillment."

"I'm done with lovers!"

"No!" he will say holding up her chart. "There will be a lot of them."

She had just resigned herself to becoming a better breadwinner and mother to Ailis and bid adieu to half-filled notebooks and men. In fact, she had hoped he would rather have quelled her artistic pretensions and romantic hopes and told her to get on with life sensibly without them. He had at least agreed that she did need to make more money.

"*Mais oui*, we need to make our own money in this life!"

—

She walks through Luxembourg Gardens after her sessions and recalls coming there as a child enchanted by its beauty and then coming there again with Maxim and his oranges. The lanes of the park are set up for you to amble through at various possible angles. This is so well done you don't notice how cleverly you are guided about in a space that feels much grander than it is. Still, you can't walk or sit on the grass which inhibits spontaneity somewhat. There are so many paths to take just as there seem to be in life but are we so free to choose, Maebh wonders.

"Woman is love and man is culture!" Louis will say in visit number three.

'These arguments are following me everywhere,' Maebh thinks.

"Men make laws but in the wilderness there are no laws and often the most cruel succeed but in culture there are laws—not rules," he will specify—"laws!"

"But lawyers convict the wrong people all the time?"

"Laws can be discussed and adjusted. You are allowed in front of a court to explain your case. It is not a perfect system but it offers us some chance. Rules are not so gracious. If you break them you are out of the game. And nature is not kind either. The cultivated fruit tree is your friend and you can reach the fruit easily. The tree grown wild needs to be climbed and its fruit filled with worms."

"The worm filled fruit might taste better than some of the over-produced stuff you find in the supermarket." she will say. "Even culture can go too far!"

"No, the American Supermarket lets greed and fear kick in. Man succumbs to his animal nature and forgoes honour, taste and elegance in favour of profit!"

"I still think culture can go too far when it becomes convinced of its superiority over nature and so can man," Maebh will say, stuttering a little but loving the discussion. "My father says there is Apollonian war—clean and bloodless, and Dionysian war—frenzied and ready to get its hands dirty."

"Maybe but I still think all war is giving into the Dionysian!"

"But one glass of Dionysian wine is okay with a meal and more agreeable than rigidly abstaining!"

"*Touché*! My dear Maebh—a bit thin but beautifully dressed in mauve," he will say so sweetly she forgives him for calling her skinny as she forgave the last man she dated who thought her too fat.

"All the same, you must enter into the realm of culture, show more respect for the essential laws that aspire to create for all, but first yourself, a more worthwhile life. You have choices you must make with much more careful consideration. Men are brutes. I'm the first to admit it but we have done some good things with our brains and your brain is bursting—so use it. It's all written here," he will say, holding up the maze of pencil lines that is her chart.

"I'm here for you *ma chérie. Adieu!*" and she will visit him, here and there, for years to come.

The summer sun comes out full in Luxembourg just as she sits on one of those metal lean back chairs spread out haphazardly about the gardens. She has nowhere to rush off to and sits down with a sigh like she hasn't in years. She continues to study the little lanes and flower beds and lean back chairs. The randomness of how the chairs are placed compensates for the structured neatly weaving paths and their flower beds. She sits in the kind of half-shady spot under the trees she favours where she can enjoy the flickering sun. She looks through her shoulder bag and pulls out the Marguerite Duras book—*L'Amant*—Djamila bought for her birthday. *The Lover*—is that what woman is?

"It's brilliant!" she had told Djamila.

"Why didn't you read it before?" Djamila had asked.

"I don't read women writers."

"Oh! You are such an asshole!"

Days taken up with teaching and cooking and all her fault for rushing into marriage and a baby with the wrong man. An hour here and there but she hadn't written much, even before she had Ailis. She pulls out her daytimer which has replaced her notebook but still has some pretty little phrases.

'Maybe women can write? Maybe I'm just paralyzed?' she thinks and she lets her books fall open on her lap as the late afternoon sun comes in on an angle full on her face. She still prefers to let the words wander through her mind high above pen and paper.

A cool looking older woman walks by with two little girls. Her face displays great joy - as if motherhood has transformed her life in all the best ways - and her daughters are well behaved but she wonders if it is the little girls' great dream to grow up spending their days taking children of their own to the park every day and this makes Maebh feel suffocated.

Ailis is with JC and his girlfriend and Maebh has taken a few weeks' holiday except she is trying to remember what a holiday is—maybe she never knew. Ailis isn't missing her and her voice sounded so happy on the phone. Maebh doesn't miss Ailis either except how she wraps her arms and legs tight round as she jumps up to greet her at after school pick up. Her love for life and seeming happiness are the miracle that ease away at Maebh's lack of it. Ailis knows what she wants too while Maebh never has. She had had a temper tantrum one evening and the next morning Maebh had found her giggling to herself.

"Why are you laughing Ailis?" Maebh had asked.

"I was so angry yesterday and I screamed a lot!"

"That's true!"

"But I didn't want to cry."

"Well, why would you need to cry."

"To get what I really want."

"You don't need tears to get what you really want."

"But screaming doesn't work."

"Well, you could try just asking with a normal voice."

"Oh! I could try just asking," she had said. "But what's a normal voice?" So Maebh had acted the three voices out for her and Ailis had nodded her head.

"But what if you say no?" she had said.

"If Mummy says no, it's not good for you and you have to accept that."

"But what if I think it is good?"

"Then we can discuss it but no screaming or whining either and I might even change my mind."

And Ailis had opened her eyes wide and hugged her and said, "I thought you were not very smart Mummy but you are smart."

"Thank you Ailis, but sometimes it's true, I'm not very smart!"

'Perhaps!' Maebh thinks as the sun goes down and the air turns cool, 'the bad choices can be forgiven as part of the way of things?'

She walks out the park, towards La Chapelle and over Le Pont des Arts, stopping mid-way just a second to ponder the Seine which is not as pretty close up as the Vltava. On the Charles Bridge in Prague summers ago she had let JC into her life to look at what she knew to know it better.

The wooden planks of the bridge shift here and there under her feet and she catches a glimpse of the bits of plastic and plantlife slipping beneath her on the miry waters—barely discernible but there like all that has transpired.

She meanders through Tuileries. The walls of the Louvre have been cleaned but most Parisian buildings are still darkened with soot. There aren't as many nude women pasted about either. You can feel the pride and elegance resonating through the city stronger than ever especially since the World Cup took over last summer and France won. Every street crammed with even the most pessimistic "they'll-never-win" Parisian. Red, white and blue and the chants of *trois zéro.* The summer before, the death of Princess Diana in the Pont de l'Alma tunnel had put a pall on the seedier exuberance of the city. Maebh has witnessed these things and Paris is hers. Change is part of you, beyond yourself, and there's so much else to see you survive.

"Almost *dix ans en Europe!*" she says to herself noticing again that her thoughts have been taken over by a kind of franglais. "I am in exile like I've never felt more *chez moi.* My *pauvre français* has reached an everyday fluency and *mon anglais* is all mixed up."

Dubi had visited last summer too and had stayed with her. It had been so nice to see him cleaned up in a slick black T-shirt, grey dress pants and brand new flowery Vans sneakers, his red curls slightly muddier and tamed now. He had just gotten his first writing job in film and was still trying to get one of his own up and going.

"Toronto was really rough for a while after university," he had said. "There wasn't any work for Lit. Studies and Philosophy grads and nobody liked my "gay" little film."

"It was like that already before I left," she had said. "It's like that here too."

"Yeah! Anyway, one day I got so fed up I decided to kill myself!"

"No!"

"Yeah, I managed to stay off the heroine but reality is brutal and I just didn't know what to do with myself so I picked up a knife and started cutting my neck. It didn't work and I just kept cutting and cutting but it hurt so much."

"Oh my god!"

"And so then I finally just went into Dad's bedroom bleeding all over the place and asked him to take me to hospital."

"Dubi!"

"They put me on drugs—ha ha!" he had said. "The legal kind and I got some crap money job in film and have been fine ever since."

"Poor you!" Maebh had said.

Dubi had roughed up his hair a bit awkwardly, stopped clutching at his legs and looked more like his old self. They had sat curled up together on Maebh's clic-clac couch sipping their wine with the bit of steak and green beans Maebh had made.

"It's French diet food!" she had said slobbering butter and parsley over everything. "Don't you love it!"

"Yeah, but some frites would be nice!"

That Portishead song everyone is listening to comes on. It takes down walls as some songs do and it's as if all the years they had forgotten each other contract as do the negative associations they had of them. Nobody in Audrey Hepburn gloves would have been singing about needing a reason to be a woman back then though, Maebh had thought.

"Anyway, Maebh!" Dubi had said as they started dancing. "We are all messed up and Toronto is as bland as ever but if you want to come back, we would not think badly of you and would all be there to support you."

"I'm never going back to Canada!"

They had started singing the song together, wine glasses out over their heads and even put it on replay a few times. Dubi looked contained, even with all the wine, and not at all like someone who had tried to "off" himself but Maebh wished she could reach out somehow to him and had raised her hand to stroke his face but they have never been close enough for that and Maebh had realized she has never been close—as close as humanly possible—to anyone except maybe her daughter who was sleeping soundly, as she always did through Maebh's soirées. As close as humanly possible? Hmn! Maybe she had been with Maxim for a short time. And what did it mean, she thought—the giving up of oneself to another for mutual contentment. The mutual part or knowing when someone was deserving, being something Maebh would take another two decades to comprehend. It was something you had to keep trying over and over till it made sense.

Dubi had poured himself another glass and moved over to the window which was wide open over Paris to contemplate the city lights.

"*Ça va être chaud!*" he had said in perfect private school French.

"Jesus Dubi!" she had said again going over to him, putting her arm awkwardly over his shoulder and trying not to stare at the deep ugly scar on his neck or wonder what all that cutting must have felt like. "I am so damn happy you are here!"

She takes a slight detour through Palais-Royale which now has a black and white series of short columns in the courtyard. She could walk up Boulevard de l'Opéra home but her feet decide they have other plans and take her back over the river again to Saint-Michel. She sees Notre Dame on her left and decides to face the tourists and go into Shakespeare & Co. She has been ignoring this bookshop since she went there with Maxim but the pale pink sunset passes timeless clear across Paris and it's like she has just arrived.

Ulysses is of course propped up on the second shelf. This is where Joyce had it published and she thinks about how Molly and Poldy accept their respective infidelities and curios and find a way to love each other through it. JC, she thinks, could never have loved with that kind of humanity however much of a Bloom man he took himself for.

She wanders upstairs through the tiny rooms. Someone is playing Erik Satie on the piano—a piece that Maebh had once tried to play—a small Asian woman with smaller hands than Maebh but somehow she is able to stretch her fingers out over nine notes in a way Maebh never could. The music lifts up—light, precise and all the Americans and Australians in the packed room sit hushed.

'My body has always been so stiff and maybe the rest of me is too,' Maebh thinks going back downstairs.

She sees a book by the woman who wrote the essay Djamila gave her a few weeks ago. *Sexual Personae by* Camille Paglia and she buys it. The book is thick and starts with Nefertiti and ends with Emily

Dickinson. Her whole self is burning hot with it in her hands as she puts it in her bag with the Marguerite Duras and her anxiety about women and success dissipates somewhat with the weight of the accomplishments of these women dragging on her right shoulder.

"Have you read Virginia Woolf?" the bookseller asks.

"Yes!" she lies to avoid explaining why not.

She feels her phone ringing in her bag. It's Djamila! She's called five times!

"I love knowing I can reach you," she says.

"Aw!" Maebh says.

"Are you coming by tomorrow for dinner? Bertrand has a block of foie gras."

"Oh yes!"

Djamila and Bertrand just moved into a place together near the Canal Saint-Martin which is a much cooler 'hood than it was when Maebh and JC stayed in the broom closet there back in the day.

"I've finished my film."

"Did you find all the women you needed to interview?"

"I decided to just use my mother."

"That's sweet!"

"She's still angry but has had such an interesting life and says the circumcision almost drove her ambition further to become a gynaecologist but she also admits she doesn't want to give in to self pity either so she tries not to think about it."

"Life does work in strange ways. Sex is so damn confusing sometimes I wish I had just become a nun as I wanted to as a child," Maebh says."But I know I would have been chickening out somehow."

"You mean you would have been kicked out more like."

"Fine! Anyway congrats on the film!"

"It's just a short." she says.

"No! It's huge!" Maebh says. "And I'm jealous!"

"Renaud will be at the dinner." Djamila says.

"It didn't work out!"

"Why not?"

"He showed up every night at midnight for action and I have to wake up daisy fresh to mother and teach at 7."

"Well, Ailis isn't even here now so why don't you give him another chance."

"Alright!" Renaud had insisted that small breasts have their charm and they had written poems together.

"Try not to be weird okay!"

"Well, that's who I am."

"I told him to take it slow with you and caress you tons."

"You did what?"

"It's what you need."

"How do you know?"

"I just do!"

"How's it going with Bertrand?"

"Ugh! we fight about money all the time and are both getting fat."

"That's kind of cute!"

"By the way, can you lend me five hundred francs again?"

"What about your Allocation Spectacle?"

"Burnt through it!"

"Shit!" Maebh says. "I really can't!"

"Damn, I'll have to buy some clothes on my Visa and take them back for cash then."

"I thought Bertrand was starting a new job with Gallimard."

"He still has to finish the copy-editing course."

"I bought that book by Camille Paglia you recommended," Maebh says to change the subject because the last time she lent Djamila money Maebh had had to chase her down for it.

"Who's Camille Paglia?"

"You know the woman who wrote that essay about the '*chthonian*.'"

"Are you still going on about all that?" asks Djamila.

"I'm still trying to get to the bottom of the woman is nature and man is culture thing."

"Maybe that's just how it is."

"But what about male desire and rage?"

"Well, I think it is like the yin yang really," Djamila says.

"But then why make it masculine and feminine?"

"They are just components."

"But society forgets that part."

"Yeah!"

"I mean Poseidon is the sea—and Athena is war, Zeus is thunder and Hestia is the hearth, Demeter is agriculture. There's as much culture in the feminine as there's nature in the masculine and isn't culture that perfect spot between nature and something else?"

"Culture is ... I have no idea—wait doesn't Paglia talk more about the Apollonian and Dionysian and I almost forgot, what happened with the astrologer?" she says. "Anyway, I'll see you for dinner tomorrow!"

"I'll bring champagne," Maebh says.

Maebh crosses Pont Notre-Dame to Châtelet, and along Rue de Rivoli to Pyramides and up Boulevard de l'Opéra to the metro which will take her straight to Saint-Lazare where she can transfer direct to Mairie de Clichy. The evening pinks swish deeper mauve and golden too over the sky. Maebh's bag is heavy and she hates more than ever living on the other side of the *Périphérique* but her feet keep moving.

She can't remember where she heard about that male, female, nature, culture stuff or perhaps it was just absorbed. She really is on the fringe of the fringe—a tired, blumbling knower of nothing.

Her parents are moving back to Toronto. Mum came off a bit *culchie* in Dublin and wants to go back to real estate and Dad is annoyed at how right wing the newspaper is getting and he doesn't trust that Tony Blair.

"I've got reporters covering atrocities all over the world but they won't let me print what's really going on," her father had said.

Roisin and James are in Toronto too. Sinead who never left is making her way up the movie business chain and got Roisin a PA job. Maebh might go back one day—back to the University of Toronto and put Ailis in French school.

Maebh could walk still further to Saint-Lazare and she even thinks about going into the Galeries Lafayette to check out the sales but her feet are done in and it's closed. Anyway, she has completely refurbished her wardrobe since JC threw it all away, clawing at whatever he could see of her.

"You've really found your style," the saleslady at the boutique in Montmartre had said and Maebh is happy she feels herself on the outside at least, even if a stiffness within her suggests more is at stake.

'Nice clothes, a job, a boho pad and Ailis is happy—maybe it's time to make a mess somewhere else!' Maebh thinks and tomorrow she will eat a whole block of expertly-chilled foie gras with a perfect bottle of perfectly-chilled champagne in Djamila and Bertrand's new kitchen. Bertrand will slice it thin on thin pieces of pain Poilâine they toast with the toaster right on the table. They eat slice by slice as it's ready—the bread for each slice hot and soft and the foie gras which you mustn't spread still chill and firmly holding its shape. She'll give Renaud, who brought her some daisies, another try—for a week—but they have nothing much to say to each other.

"It's not even Christmas," Djamila says and "don't you love the view over the canal. You can see it through the courtyard if you stand on tip-toe from the kitchen window."

"That's why I'm serving it with these caramelized peaches," Bertrand says scooping out three or four slices cut an eighth thick—golden and sweet—onto some frieze on each of their plates.

The night sets in as Maebh walks down the metro steps at Opéra laughing to herself. There's a FNAC ad for Alanis Morrisette, the Canadian singer she has heard people talking about. Canada feels so far away. Apparently at one point, they even had a female prime minister and Maebh never knew her name. She walks up the platform trying to not let the women with laundry detergent ad make her angry, wondering if nature held women back or man's need to categorize. But her head gets stuck in the weight of her own life—Ailis and JC and love and family and what for, and then does it all come to a purpose, and when she walks by an ad for moules frites, to thoughts of dinner.

She takes out her apple on the metro platform at Saint-Lazare—no it's a pear and not too mushy or bruised by some miracle wrapped carefully in a small napkin. Faded green the skin and faded pink the flesh. The metro odours drift in—piss mostly—and the platform is still busy and she might not get a seat so she waits till she gets outside at Mairie de Clichy before she takes her first bite.

The moon is out now and Maebh can even see a star or maybe it's Venus. She marvels at the illusory calm overhead—the night movements so carefully placed through light and shade and time. Nature has its own instinct towards survival. It breeds awe, which breeds love, which breeds culture and as such it finds balance and symmetry—at least from afar—otherwise it would be crashing madness up there, or maybe it is. Her throat opens up, in the hum of experience, to words she may never find.

'And the stars, are they male and female, do the females shine less bright, can they feel my shame?'

The pear needs a bit of ripening but is sweet and fresh and has good crunch. On the Rue Villeneuve, she holds this in hand to digest.

Acknowledgements

Thank you:

Grande Luciano Iacobelli and Quattro for publishing this book. Bilal Hasmi for the copyedits, Jared Shapiro for the book design x2 and Alireza Atarian for the corset image. Robin Richardson and David Layton for the life changing mentorship and edits.

Antonio D'Alfonso, Marina Nemat, Dennis Boch, Michelle Berry, Erica de Vasconcelos, Sam Solecki and DM Thomas for your insights. All the many writers in writing groups I've worked with over the years; Alexandra Bednar, Concetta Principe, Joyce Wayne, Paola Ferrante and Ian Burgham most of all.

David Cowper-Smith for going above and beyond to negotiate academic leave so I could write the book, Martine Allard for approving it and my lovely Seneca College students and colleagues esp. Arif Anwar, Vesna Vekujicic-Ristic, Jean Nielsen, Carole Pye, Ross McCague and Sophia Tang. Friends in Paris, Anna Oliel, Mayana von Ledebur, Beatrice Percival, Francois Boisivon, Pierre Lasserre, Gilles D'Ambra (I have not forgotten you). Didier Betournié for seeing stars and the Mairie de Paris for giving us dignity.

All my many friends - Ewan Whyte, Salma Bani, Robert Delaney, Cornelia Principe, Zeen Boeghel, Becky Upfold, Ayah Victoria McPhail, Renee Logan, Giovanna Filippi, Vladimir Azarov, David Logan, Kimeiko Hotta Dover, Louise Gywn, Tim Owen, Mehernaz Lentin, Stéphane Beauroy. Paul Dore, Dihan Chandratne and the CSI. Bahar Biazar, blazing queen of justice and grace, for keeping the steady smile on my face.

Mum and Dad who always had room for the prodigal at their table, brother Ed for his helping hand and Shauna and Fionnuala, sisters in crime for doing everything loving sisters should. My children, Alice and Seamus, whose love and innocence made this book necessary and Alessandro Bruno who read each and every draft and loved them as me, in all apparitions.

About the Author

Siobhan Jamison teaches at Seneca College in Toronto. *Maternity and Other Corsets* is her first book and she is writing its follow-up, *Frozen Meat on Hooks.*